Darkness...

Broken, she thought.

Broken, broken, broken.

And it will never be put back together again.

The rain continued to batter the wide double windows behind them.

The lights flickered again.

Darkness, Abby thought. Soon we will all be cast into darkness.

The lights flickered and went out.

Matches were struck by shaking hands. Circles of yellow candle light cast an eerie, old-fashioned glow.

Abby stared into Leila's candle flame.

"One of us is a killer," she said.

Other Point paperbacks by R.L. STINE
you will enjoy:

TWISTED

R.L. STINE

SCHOLASTIC INC.

New York Toronto London Auckland Sydney

No part of this publication may be reproduced in whole or in part, or stored in a retrieval system, or transmitted in any form or by any means, electronic, mechanical, photocopying, recording, or otherwise, without written permission of the publisher. For information regarding permission, write to Scholastic Inc., 730 Broadway, New York, NY 10003.

ISBN 0-590-43139-0

21 20 19 18 17 16 15 14   4 5 6 7 8/9

Printed in the U.S.A.   01

Chapter 1

"I really don't believe you, Gabriella."

Abby stared into the mirror. Gabriella's reflection gave her a disdainful sneer.

"How can you turn your nose up at the Tri Gams?" Abby asked. "You know, most girls would *kill* to get into this sorority."

Gabriella's expression didn't change. "I'm just not interested," she said.

Abby picked up a lipstick and began to rub it with short, quick strokes across her already red lips. "The Tri Gams are the most exclusive sorority at Rockland State," she said, stopping to admire her work. "They only pledge ten girls a year. It's an honor to be asked, Gabriella."

She stared into the mirror, waiting for Gabriella to react. "Aren't you going to say anything?"

Gabriella only shrugged.

A flash of anger made Abby's pale, white skin turn scarlet. Why did Gabriella always make her feel like a chattering ten-year-old?

What made her think she was so superior?

She certainly wasn't as pretty as Abby. And she wasn't as smart either, Abby decided. Sneering at an invitation to pledge the Tri Gamma Sorority was just plain stupid. And spiteful.

Still angry, Abby picked up her hairbrush. She removed a piece of lint from the bristles and began brushing her straight, black hair, still staring at Gabriella. "This is the best haircut I ever got," she said. "Don't you think so?"

"It's a little short," Gabriella said, frowning. "Hard to get used to."

"Thanks a bunch," Abby snapped, brushing furiously. "Can't you say *anything* nice? What's wrong with you today, Gabriella?"

Now it was Gabriella who angrily turned red. "Don't start with me, Abby. There's nothing wrong with *me*. If you want to go to that sorority house and let yourself be judged by a group of superficial snobs — that's *your* business. But don't try to make me feel like *I'm* twisted or something just because I don't want to spend all my time at college talking about clothes and worrying about who's going to take me to the party after the football game on Saturday night!"

Abby let out a hurt gasp. She knew she shouldn't let Gabriella get to her. She knew she should just let the conversation drop. But it was too late. And she was too upset. It had been so long since Abby had had any good news. Why was Gabriella trying to spoil it for her?

"So *that's* it," Abby said, slamming down the hairbrush and glaring into the mirror. "You're afraid, aren't you, Gabriella! You're afraid to be judged. You're not going to pledge the Tri Gams because you're afraid you might not be accepted."

Gabriella glared right back. She had the same olive, catlike eyes as Abby. With her round, high-cheekboned face framed by her short, black hair, and with her soft, silent, graceful walk, Abby reminded some people of a cat. No one ever thought of Gabriella as a cat. Gabriella was a tiger. . . .

"*I'm* not afraid to test myself," Gabriella replied through clenched teeth. "*I'm* the confident one, remember? I *know* what I want. And what *I* want isn't at the Tri Gam house."

Abby felt herself losing control, felt the muscles in her neck tighten, felt the tears well up in her eyes. Why did she always let Gabriella get to her like this? "Sure, Gabriella — you're always so confident, so calm, so certain about everything!" she screamed. "It's inhuman. That's what it is. You're inhuman!"

A cold silence fell between them. Abby shuddered and looked down at her dressing table.

"What a nice thing to say to a sister," Gabriella said bitterly.

Abby didn't look up. The back of her neck felt hot. Her hands were ice cold. "I don't care. *I'm* going to pledge Tri Gamma, and I'm going to be accepted, and I'm going to move out of here, and I'm going to have a new life, a *great* life. . . ."

She spun around quickly, but Gabriella had left.

"Hey — what's going on up here?"

Abby's mother stepped into the bedroom, frowning. She removed a tissue from the pocket of her white uniform and dabbed at her nose.

"Nothing. I'm just getting dressed for the pledge meeting," Abby said, turning back to the mirror. As she watched her mother in the mirror, she realized she liked to talk to people's reflections. It was easier somehow. "Did you get another cold?"

Mrs. Wallis nodded, the tissue still pressed against her nose. "That's the problem with being a nurse," she said. "You get everything your patients have."

Abby stood up and faced her mother. It was a little like looking in a mirror. Her mother looked a lot like her, except that her olive eyes were set in dark rings of weariness, and her black hair was streaked with gray and pulled tightly back to fit under her nurse's cap.

"Well . . . how do I look?" Abby asked, performing a graceful curtsey.

"Your sweater tag is up. Let me fix it for you," her mother said. She shoved the tissue back into her pocket and started toward Abby.

But Abby stepped away. "Can't you ever say anything nice?" she snapped, sounding more angry than she had intended.

Her mother's mouth dropped open in surprise. "What?"

"I've been up here for over an hour getting myself ready for something that's very important to me, and all you can say is, 'Your tag is up.'"

Her mother closed her eyes and kept them shut for a few seconds. "Sorry," she said. She opened them and smiled. "You look great, Abby."

"I'm sorry, too," Abby said quickly, looking back toward the mirror. "I didn't mean to yell at you. I guess I'm just nervous."

"Getting into this sorority means a lot to you, doesn't it?" her mother asked, wiping her nose with the tissue again.

"Yeah," Abby said softly. "A lot."

"Well, I'll miss you if you go to live in that sorority house. The house will seem really empty without you."

"I'll only be half an hour away, mother." Abby didn't mean to sound so annoyed. Why did her voice sound so strained, so harsh?

"I know. I know," Mrs. Wallis said, sighing. She sat down on the edge of Abby's bed, looking tired and pale.

"Don't sit down. I'm leaving," Abby said, forcing herself not to sound impatient. But she was dying to get out of the house and to the campus.

"Abby..."

"What *is* it, mother? I really don't have time to — "

"I just want to ask you . . . uh . . . I mean . . , if you don't get in . . . if the sorority turns you down . . . do you think you can handle it?"

Abby laughed. She wasn't sure why. "Mother — stop. They're not going to reject me. I'm going to get in — no matter what."

She took one last look into the mirror, and walked past her mother, down the narrow stairway, and out into the street.

Chapter 2

Abby gazed out the bus window, watching the evening fog billow around the houses she passed. She shivered. Living in a town so near the ocean always meant a September of fog and chill. Car headlights seemed unable to penetrate the shifting curtain of fog. A mist of gray-green light danced eerily along the quiet street.

The houses were all familiar to Abby, even in the fog. She had lived in North Shore Village her entire life. She knew every house, every two-car garage, every tree and carefully trimmed hedge on this street. Even in the mysterious, swirling light, it all looked familiar, pieces of the world she knew too well, the world she hoped to leave behind.

The campus of Rockland State was only a half-hour bus ride from her house, but it seemed like a new world to Abby. The ivy-covered red brick buildings facing onto the wide, grassy quadrangle, the new courses, the new faces — all seemed to offer a fresh start, a new beginning, a world where Abby had no past, only a promising future.

The bus stopped a block from the Tri Gam house, and Abby stepped out into the cold, wet air. She walked quickly past the row of campus shops that led toward Greek Row. The bookstore was still open. Through the window she could see a boy from her Comp. Lit. class carefully looking through a stack of used textbooks.

She hurried past the bookstore, past Ernie's Coffee Shop, past the tiny jewelry store with the sign in the window: EARS PIERCED WHILE-U-WAIT.

Why was it so freezing cold? She knew she should have worn a coat or a heavier sweater, but that wasn't the look she wanted for her first appearance in the Tri Gam house. Her oversized gold sweater, and short, brown knit skirt over dark, patterned tights were just the right choice, she told herself — sophisticated, sexy, but casual.

Casual? Abby had to laugh at the thought. She had spent two hours trying to decide what to wear. This decision was anything but casual!

And why should she be casual about something that meant so much to her? First impressions are important. She didn't want everyone's first impression of her to be of someone all bundled up against the cold.

She was halfway across the street before

she realized she hadn't looked for traffic. Luckily, the street was empty except for a pizza delivery boy on a bike. He looked her up and down as he pedaled past.

I guess I chose the right outfit, Abby thought, smiling.

The Beta house, with its tall wrought-iron fence that made it look like some kind of prison, stood on the corner. Abby began to walk faster. The Tri Gam house was next, just beyond a row of shedding oak trees.

She looked across the lawn to the entrance. A white spotlight pierced the fog, illuminating the twin white columns that framed the stairway. The white double doors beyond the stairway were pulled open.

Abby stumbled over a stone on the sidewalk. She quickly recovered her balance. Take it easy, Abby, she told herself. Just stay calm, girl. But *saying* it was a lot easier than *doing* it.

Another girl stepped into the light of the spotlight, about to enter the sorority house. Abby stopped. Her heart seemed to stop. She shivered, this time not from the cold.

It was Leila. Leila Sherman.

She watched Leila enter the house, then stood staring at the open doors behind the two white columns. Leila Sherman was pledging the Tri Gams, too? How could that be??

For a moment, Abby thought of turning around and going home. She felt somehow betrayed, invaded. Leila was part of the past. What right did she have to enter Abby's new world?

It doesn't matter, Abby told herself. Leila doesn't matter anymore. Past is past.

So why did she feel so crummy?

Abby had heard that Leila was still going with Gordon, even though he wasn't in school.

"Well, she's welcome to him," Abby said, and then realized she was talking out loud. Embarrassed, she looked around quickly to make sure no one had heard her.

The Tri Gams aren't likely to accept a pledge who talks to herself on the street, she thought, forcing a smile to her tight lips.

Past is past.

It had been a year, a whole year, since the thing with Leila and Gordon. She hadn't spoken to either of them for a year.

So why did she still feel so crummy?

She couldn't ignore the question. She *had* to ignore the question.

"Gordon's a creep." She was talking out loud again. He wasn't in college. He had just barely graduated with their class at North Shore High. He didn't have a job. As far as Abby knew, he wasn't doing *anything*.

Except going with Leila.

Abby stamped her foot angrily against the sidewalk.

Enough.

She tried to force all of these thoughts, all of these memories from her mind.

Enough. Enough. Enough.

Was she going to walk into the Tri Gam house?

Yes.

Was she going to wow them with her good looks, her sophistication, her ready intelligence?

Yes.

Was she going to forget all about Leila and Gordon, and let bygones be bygones?

Maybe....

When she took her first steps through the entranceway to the Tri Gam house, Abby expected to enter a vibrant and sparkling new world. At first glance, however, the new world was less than sparkling. In fact, it was pretty rundown.

The flowered wallpaper was peeling in the entrance hallway. The faded green corduroy armchairs Abby saw as she sneaked a peek into the living room were worn and had yellow stuffing coming out of their cushions.

The Tri Gam who greeted her at the doorway *was* wearing a trendy designer jumpsuit. But she had a clump of green stuff stuck to her front tooth, and her smile was plastered on as if she had been *forced* to be the official greeter.

Abby forced a smile of her own and shook the girl's slender hand.

"Ooooh — your hand is freezing," the Tri

Gam cried, without losing her smile. "Why didn't you wear a coat?"

Then Abby, her confidence just about completely shaken, was handed a name tag and directed up the stairs to the meeting room. A few rows of folding chairs had been set up facing a music stand at the front of the room. A hand-stenciled sign on the wall said:

GAMMA GAMMA GAMMA
WELCOME ITS PLEDGES.

She saw Leila across the room, her blonde hair pulled to the side in a long, stylish braid, concentrating on getting the name tag to stick to her clinging, wine-colored sweaterdress.

Past is past.

Abby looked away from Leila quickly. She wanted to calm down, to get more comfortable before approaching her.

Two girls Abby had never seen before were talking nearby, gesturing nervously with their hands and laughing too quickly at everything being said. Grateful that she and Leila weren't the only ones in the room, Abby started over to join them.

"Abby! Hey — Abby!"

A familiar voice. Abby turned around quickly. "Nina!"

"What are *you* doing here?"

"What are *you* doing here?"

They laughed.

"I don't *believe* it!"

"I don't *believe* it!"

"Hey, stop — " Abby said, grabbing hold

of Nina's shoulder. "If we're both going to say the same things, one of us has to talk and the other listen."

"You go first," Nina said in her scratchy little voice. "I haven't seen you in ages!"

With her short hair still in bangs, her tiny stub of a nose, no makeup at all, and freckles dotting her cheeks, Nina looked about ten years old. Abby realized she had known Nina since they were both ten, and Nina hadn't changed much at all!

They had been inseparable when they were little girls. But the friendship had struggled through junior high. And by the time they reached high school, Nina just seemed too giggly, too silly, too naive, too *young* for cool, controlled Abby, and they never saw each other away from school.

Nina became a cheerleader, was president of the Pep Club, and had pinup pictures of rock stars taped to her locker door. Abby became feature editor of the newspaper, wrote long, surreal poems for the literary magazine ... and fell in love with Gordon.

Whenever Abby passed Nina in the halls at North Shore High, she would wonder what they had ever found to talk about when they were younger. But now, standing nervously near the wall of the Tri Gam meeting room with Leila looking at her from across the room, Abby was genuinely glad to see Nina.

"I'm so happy you're pledging, too. It's great to see you. I haven't seen you on campus.

Where are you living? Are you at home or are you in a dorm, or what?" Abby asked without taking a breath.

Nina giggled, the same giggle she had had when she was ten. "Abby — did you take a speed-talking course?!"

They both laughed. Somehow Nina's joke made Abby feel a little calmer.

"I'm in the dorm — Copley Hall," Nina said, looking past Abby as two more worried-looking pledges entered the room. "It's really great!"

Great . . . great . . . Abby thought. Hasn't she learned a *new* word yet? But she smiled warmly, scolding herself for thinking such mean thoughts.

"Leila's my roommate," Nina chirped. "Isn't that great?" She wrinkled her nose and grinned. "I just think it's *amazing* that three girls from North Shore High are pledging the Tri Gams! Leila and you. . . ." Nina's face suddenly froze and her expression changed to embarrassment. "Oh — Abby — I'm sorry. I forgot about . . . you and Gordon."

Abby forced a fast, tight-lipped smile. "Hey — it's okay. That was a long time ago. I'm all over that." If only she could get her voice to stop shaking.

"Really? You *mean* that? Oh. Good," Nina said uncomfortably, glancing across the room at Leila, who was talking to a tall redhaired girl in a bright green Benetton sweater.

"I guess Leila and Gordon are still together," Abby said, looking at the wall, hoping that sounded casual.

"Yeah," Nina said, shrugging her tiny shoulders. "Gordon's been kinda bummed out, though. Oh — not because of Leila. Just because he can't decide what he wants to do."

"Oh." Abby couldn't think of anything else to say.

Nina shifted her weight uneasily. She smiled. A few seconds of silence passed. "Well . . . I guess I'll go sit down. It's *great* to see you. I think it's so *amazing* we're all going to be — Hey — where are you living? Are you at home?"

"Uh-huh."

"Great. Great. Well . . . uh. . . ." Nina wanted to end the conversation, but she was having trouble figuring out how. "How . . . how about coffee after the meeting?" It was a half-hearted invitation.

"Sure," Abby said quickly. "If it isn't too late."

"See ya later." Nina flashed an uncertain grin and turned away.

Abby suddenly wanted to grab onto Nina and plead with her not to go. She didn't want to have to face Leila. She didn't want to talk to Leila. Not yet.

But Nina was already talking to a couple of girls near the window. And Leila had finished her conversation with the tall redhead, and was starting to walk down the row of chairs toward Abby, a confident smile on her dark red lips.

"Hey, Abby. What a shock! Hi!"

Abby could feel her face grow hot. She knew she must be blushing bright red. It was such an embarrassing trait. She positively hated that feeling of being out of control, having her face do something that she didn't will it to do.

What was she going to say to Leila after all this time? What *could* she say? Should she be nice to her? Should she act as if nothing had happened?

"Hey, Abby — how ya doin?"

Chapter 3

"Okay, guys — let's all take seats. I think we can get started."

Abby looked toward the front of the room. A girl had stepped behind the music stand and was gesturing for everyone to sit down. "C'mon — seats, people!"

Saved by the bell, she told herself.

She looked back at Leila, who was still halfway across the room, and shrugged. "Later!" she called to her, trying to look disappointed rather than relieved.

"Sit down, people! Let's get started!"

Abby stepped quickly to the nearest row and dropped into the seat next to the tall redhaired girl in the bright green sweater. "Hi," the girl said quickly. "I'm Rebecca Reeves." She had a tiny mouse voice. At first, Abby thought it was a put-on. But she quickly realized it was Rebecca's real voice.

"Abby Wallis," Abby said, finding it hard not to imitate Rebecca's squeaky little voice. A quick handshake ended the conversation, as the girl behind the music stand began to speak.

"Let me begin by introducing myself," she said loudly, leaning on the music stand and looking around the room. "My name is Andrea Volner, and I am this year's president of Gamma Gamma Gamma."

Perfect, Abby thought. Andrea looks like the perfect president of a sorority.

Andrea wasn't exactly a cliché, but she came very close to it. She was tall and pretty, with standard American good looks, blonde hair that fell perfectly straight to just above her shoulders, and a perfect smile that could sell toothpaste on TV. She wore an expensive gray wool skirt and a maroon silk blouse with a gray silk scarf tied loosly around the collar. Even though she was tall and could see perfectly well over the music stand, she kept raising up on tiptoes as she spoke.

"I also have the pleasure of serving as this year's pledge officer," Andrea continued. "Before I tell you a little about the weeks to come, I'd like to introduce the other officers."

Abby tried to concentrate on what Andrea was saying, but her mind quickly wandered. Andrea's voice became an indistinct hum in the background as Abby's mind raced with thoughts of Nina, and Leila . . . and Gordon.

How was it possible that a year ago she and Leila had been best friends, closer than close? She thought of the hours and hours she had spent talking to Leila on the phone every day. They would meet after school to talk, and then hurry home so they could talk some more on the phone!

Even when Gordon entered the picture and he and Abby were spending so much time together — so much time, and not enough time — Abby still had time to talk with Leila. They talked, they laughed, they shared their real feelings, they confided. . . .

And now, it had all been ruined. Now, Abby wanted to run away. Now, Abby would do *anything* to avoid having to talk to Leila.

Anything?

Would she run away? Forget about pledging the Tri Gams?

No.

She had given up another dream because of Leila. She wouldn't give up *this* dream because of Leila, too.

"The Tri Gams are known beyond the college community for our tradition of public service. . . ." Andrea's words broke into Abby's thoughts, then faded again.

Why had she agreed so quickly to have coffee with Nina? She hadn't had a conversation of more than a few seconds with Nina since eighth grade! She wasn't *really* interested in hearing how *great* everything in Nina's life was, was she?

Abby realized she had agreed to meet Nina afterwards for only one reason. Perhaps Nina would tell her more about Gordon.

She could feel her face grow hot again. Gordon.

Past is past. Isn't it?

All that melodrama, all that craziness, all that pain — it was all behind her.

It was just seeing Nina and Leila again that was bringing back the memories, bringing back these strong feelings.

Stop it, Abby. Stop it now. She stared at Andrea, who was up on tiptoes again behind the music stand. She forced herself to listen.

"That's basically what I have to say about *us*," Andrea was saying. "Now I'd like to talk a little about what we expect from *you*."

Andrea drew a hand casually back through her straight, blonde hair and began to plunge into the next part of her well-practiced speech. But she was interrupted by a late-comer, a girl who seemed to explode into the room, a bulging, green book bag over her shoulder and a stack of sheet music under her arm.

"Sorry I'm late. My bassoon lesson ran over," the girl loudly announced to Andrea, swinging the bag around and almost hitting the girl seated closest to the door with it.

"That's okay. Take a seat, Jessie," Andrea said, not at all flustered by the interruption.

"I don't believe it," Rebecca leaned close and squeaked into Abby's ear. "Look at her. She didn't exactly dress up. She's wearing jeans — and they're not even 501's!"

Just about everyone in the room was watching Jessie as she swung the big bookbag off her shoulder, dropped it onto an empty chair, placed the sheet music carefully under the seat, pulled her blue and green wool poncho over her head revealing a crimson and gray ROCKLAND RAMS sweatshirt underneath, and plopped heavily into the chair beside her bookbag.

Jessie wasn't just under-dressed, Abby decided. Everything about her — from her bright red eyeglass frames and her unruly, mousey brown hair to her baggy jeans and loose-fitting sweatshirt, which only emphasized that she had a definite weight problem — indicated no desire to fit in with the others, no attempt to *look* like a Tri Gam!

Abby always tried hard not to judge people by their appearance. But seeing a girl who cared so *little* about her appearance turning up as a pledge in the Tri Gam house was certainly a shock.

"How did she get chosen?" Abby whispered to Rebecca. "Is she a fabulous bassoon player or something?"

"Her older sister was a Tri Gam," Rebecca whispered back.

That explained it. Younger sisters were automatically pledged. They weren't always accepted. But they were always pledged.

"I'd like to resume by saying a few words about *your* role." Andrea started again. She had to shout. A number of whispered conversations were suddenly taking place, no doubt all of them about Jessie.

"Before you begin — " Jessie interrupted, still trying to get her bulky poncho to rest on the seat next to her.

"Yes?" Andrea asked with only a hint of impatience.

"Maybe you talked about this before I came in," Jessie said. She spoke quickly, breathing hard, as if she had run all the way. "I just wondered if you're serving food after the meeting?"

Someone in the back of the room giggled. No one else made a sound.

"We hadn't really planned to have a social hour after the meeting," Andrea said. "Since it's a weeknight, we thought everyone would have course work to do." She looked over to the other sorority officers, who were sitting, expressionless, against the far wall. "But we could get the coffee machine going, I guess. And there are cakes or something we could warm up. . . ."

"No sandwiches?" Jessie asked.

"Well . . . no. No sandwiches. If you're really hungry, Jessie, we could — "

"No," Jessie said quickly. "I just wondered. Sorry." She went back to arranging the poncho on the chair.

"Most of us have a lot of studying," Andrea continued, not quite ready to drop the subject. "How about the rest of you people?"

Most of the pledges muttered something about having papers to write. It was quickly decided that there would be no social hour this night.

Abby was truly relieved. She had no desire to stand around in a crowded room with all of the important officers of the sorority watching, and try to make small talk with Leila. She would much rather have a quick coffee down the block at Ernie's with Nina and get home.

"Well . . ." Andrea leaned against the music stand again, smiled, and resumed her speech. "I've told you a little about what makes Gamma Gamma Gamma so special. But I haven't told you quite everything." She paused, supposedly to build suspense.

Abby stifled a yawn. It was hot in the small meeting room. The heat was beginning to make her sleepy.

"As you can see," Andrea continued, "there are only ten girls in this year's pledge class. That's a very small number, a very exclusive group. And from you ten girls, I have to tell you that only five will be accepted as members."

"Gee whiz," Jessie said loudly. It was impossible to tell if she meant it as an exclamation or if she was being sarcastic.

Andrea ignored the interruption. She leaned farther up on the music stand as if trying to get closer to her audience, to speak confidentially. "When we say that the girls of

Tri Gamma sorority are special, we don't just mean that in the ordinary way. And when we say that the members of Tri Gamma are *sisters*, we don't just mean that in the ordinary way, either."

She paused again, raised up on tip toe, then slowly lowered her heels back to the floor. "We don't want Tri Gamma just to be another social club. And it isn't. The sisters of Tri Gamma are sisters for life. The members of Tri Gamma are members for *life*.

"This is a big commitment," Andrea said, speaking more and more quietly. "Not every girl is willing to make the commitment we require, the commitment for life. Not every girl *wants* to make that commitment. Those of you who do *not* will not become members of Tri Gamma. Those of you who are willing to commit yourselves totally will be accepted."

The room grew silent and still.

Andrea had everyone's rapt attention now. She spoke almost in a whisper. "Sisters for life," she repeated. "That's what we require. Sisters for life. How do we make sure we choose the right girls, the girls who want what we want, the girls who share our need of a lifetime commitment?"

"You mean we have to go through *hazing*?" Jessie called out.

"Jessie, please!" Andrea sounded irritated for the first time. "We all know that there's no hazing at Rockland State. The university banned it five years ago. Gamma Gamma

Gamma never went in for hazing anyway. A bunch of childish pranks, so superficial and silly. It's the kind of thing that gives fraternities and sororities a bad name. Oh no. We have a very different kind of test."

The room grew silent again. A car horn honked down on the street. A dog barked somewhere in the distance.

"Every year," Andrea said quietly, "we ask our pledges to share something, to share a secret that will bind them together, to share an experience that will make them sisters for life."

She stopped to clear her throat and take a drink of water from a paper cup that rested on the music stand. "Every year, we take our pledges away from the sorority house, away from the campus, to another town. And then . . ." Andrea was talking quietly now, so quietly Abby wasn't sure she heard her correctly.

"And then . . ." Andrea whispered, "to make sure you will be loyal Tri Gammas for life . . . we ask our pledges to commit a *crime.*"

Chapter 4

"She wasn't serious — *was* she?"

Nina frowned. Her forehead wrinkled whenever she was thinking hard, and the freckles around her nose seemed to wrinkle, too. "Was she?"

Abby laughed. "I don't know, Nina. I really don't."

Nina held the steaming gray coffee cup up to her lips and blew on it. She stared into Abby's eyes as if the answer to her question was somehow hidden inside them.

"Stop looking at me like that," Abby said, and laughed again. Nina was so serious about this, it was comical. "No. I don't think Andrea was serious. I don't think she really wants us to commit a crime. Is *that* what you want me to say?"

"She *is* serious!" Nina decided, setting the cup down too hard on the green formica table-top. She pulled a napkin from the dispenser and began wiping up the brown puddle of coffee she had spilled.

"You still have these tiny hands," Abby said, without thinking. As soon as she said it, she remembered that Nina was sensitive about the size of her hands.

Nina looked hurt for a second, but quickly changed her expression. "Hands don't grow," she said, tossing the wet napkin in an ashtray. "It's a scientific fact."

It's a scientific fact.

I don't believe it, Abby thought. Nina was saying that when she was ten!

Abby found herself grinning at her old friend. A flood of warm feelings rushed over her. It was good to be sitting here at Ernie's Coffee Shop on a Monday night, talking comfortably with someone she had known for so many years.

The small, dimly lit room was nearly empty. A couple of old men sat at the counter staring vacantly at the wall, their bony white hands wrapped around half-empty coffee cups. In the corner booth across the room from Abby and Nina, a boy and girl in identical denim jackets were wrapped around each other and seemed to be challenging the World's Record For The Longest Kiss. Their sandwiches sat untouched in front of them.

Abby looked back at Nina. "She *couldn't* be serious!" Nina decided, changing her mind again. "She sure *looked* serious. But she couldn't mean it, Abby. She *couldn't* expect us to commit a crime to get accepted into the sorority. Could she?"

"Whatever it is, it'll be completely harmless," Abby said. "Sororities always make their pledges do silly things. It'll be silly — that's all."

"Silly. Yeah. I'm sure you're right," Nina said. But she didn't look or sound convinced. "Hey — did you get to talk to Leila?"

"Yeah. A little." Abby forced a smile. "She said hi, and I said hi. And then some other girl asked her a question and that was that."

"She looks great, doesn't she?" Nina asked. It was her first *great* of the conversation, Abby realized. "I love what she's done to her hair. She looks just like that model — you know the one."

Abby didn't know the one, but she nodded anyway.

"Do you still keep up with all the gossip about the models and their love lives and everything?" Abby asked.

Nina giggled. "A little," she admitted guiltily. "Not as much as I used to. I don't still plan to be a famous model when I grow up, if that's what you're asking!"

They both laughed. It was a little like the old days, years ago. But then neither could think of what to say next.

"I'm a little worried about Leila," Nina said suddenly, wrinkling her forehead again.

"What do you mean?"

"Oh, I probably shouldn't say anything . . . especially to you."

Abby's heart began to pound. "It's okay,"

she said quietly, trying not to look too interested.

"Well . . . I don't know . . . it . . . it's about Leila and Gordon." Nina sipped her coffee and made a face. "Ooo — bitter."

Abby shoved the sugar container across the table to her, a little too vigorously. It almost toppled into Nina's lap, but she caught it at the table edge.

"Sorry."

Nina quickly dumped three spoons of sugar into her coffee. "I'm sure I'll like the taste of coffee *some* day," she said. "What was I talking about?"

"Leila and Gordon," Abby said, a little too loudly.

But Nina didn't seem to notice. "I just don't think Gordon is right for Leila at this point in her life," Nina said. "Here she is in her first semester at Rockland, and he's . . . he's just nowhere. No job, no school, no plans. And he doesn't seem to care. I'm just afraid he's gonna drag her down with him."

"What do you mean?" Abby asked, staring into her coffee cup. Her hands, tightly clasped in her lap, suddenly felt ice cold.

"Oh . . . well . . . I wouldn't tell you this if we all weren't such old friends. I had a study date with some kids in another dorm the other night, and I was walking back to my dorm. It was really late, after midnight. The doors close at twelve-fifteen. And I was crossing through the parking lot — you know, behind the dorm. And there was that old car that Gordon drives parked by the fence.

"I guess I was surprised to see it there so late, or something. I had to walk right by it. And as I walked by, I looked in the car. And they were there — inside, in the back seat. In the dorm parking lot — can you *imagine*?

"That parking lot is pretty well lit up. Do you know how much trouble Leila could be in if the campus cops came by, or something? She could be kicked out of school. Do you think I should say something to her? Should I — "

Nina stopped when she saw Abby's face.

Abby felt her face growing bright red. She knew there was nothing she could do about that. She struggled to get her trembling lips and chin under control. But it was a losing battle.

Abby's words came through clenched teeth in a hard, cold voice she had never heard before. "Leila's a big girl. She can take care of herself."

Startled, Nina dropped her cup onto its saucer. "Oh, I'm spilling more than I'm drinking." She reached for another paper napkin. "Listen, Abby — I'm sorry . . . really . . . I guess it was dumb of me to think — "

"No, no — " Abby started to protest, still unable to stop her quivering face.

She was just about to tell Nina to go on, to tell her more, when they were interrupted by a loud, cheerful voice.

"Well, well — so *this* is where the in-crowd hangs out! Hi!"

It was Jessie, the girl who had arrived late at the pledge meeting and had asked about the sandwiches. She dropped her bookbag to the floor and without removing her bulky poncho, began to slide uninvited next to Abby in the booth.

"You girls were at the pledge meeting — right? I'm Jessie Harvard. Like the University." She grabbed Abby's cold hand and squeezed it, then reached across the table to shake Nina's hand.

"Uh . . . I'm Nina. And this is Abby."

Abby was tempted to tell Jessie she was interrupting their conversation. As much as it was hurting her, she wanted desperately to hear more about Leila and Gordon.

But she and Nina both were reluctant to be rude to a fellow Tri Gam pledge. Besides, what would be the point? Jessie was already sitting down, already calling to the waiter behind the counter to bring her a grilled cheese and french fries, already pulling that hideous poncho over her head.

"So what do you think?" Jessie asked, grinning first at Abby, then at Nina.

They both just stared at her.

Nina was the first to recover. "Do *you* think Andrea was telling the truth? Do you think the crime thing is for real?"

Jessie raised an ink-stained finger to her lips. "Shhhh. We're not supposed to talk

31

about it — remember?" she said loudly. She seemed incapable of talking below a shout.

"I know," Nina whispered. "But what do you think?"

Jessie raised her head and looked around the coffee shop. The two old men had climbed off their stools and were standing in front of the broken Pac-Man machine in the back. The couple in the back booth still had their lips glued together.

"I think it's gonna happen," Jessie said, smiling. "And I can't wait!" Her dull, gray eyes suddenly lit up. "I've always dreamed of pulling off some kind of heist. Maybe getting into a big chase scene. Do you think we'll get to use guns?"

"Are you for *real*?" Nina blurted out. She was sorry immediately that she had said it. After all, she didn't know Jessie at all.

Jessie didn't seem at all taken aback by the question. Abby figured that people asked her that question all the time!

"Haven't you ever wanted to live a fantasy?" Jessie asked. "To live another life — a *wild* life — a life of adventure, of *crime*? Haven't you ever dreamed of doing something — bad — *really bad*? Well, here comes our chance!"

Good lord, thought Abby. This girl is definitely twisted. She's so excited about committing a crime, she's practically drooling on the table!

Abby looked at her watch. "Hey — it's getting late. I told my mom I'd be home, so..."

"You live at home? So do I," Jessie said, her face still animated from talking about the crime they were going to commit. "Where'd you go to school?"

"North Shore," Abby said, looking at Nina.

"Oh. I went to South Shore," Jessie said, a little defensively. South Shore was the less affluent of the two villages, populated largely by the people who worked for the home-owners in North Shore.

"Yeah. Guess we'd better be going," Nina said, getting up quickly and pulling her jacket on.

"Oh. Okay," Abby agreed, a bit too enthusiastically.

"Gee, I just got here," Jessie said, disappointed. She slowly pulled herself out of the booth so that Abby could slide out. "Well ... nice meeting you two."

"Nice meeting you," Abby and Nina called back. They were already hurrying out the door.

They stepped out onto the sidewalk. The air smelled fresh and cool. They looked at each other and started laughing.

"*She's* going to be a *Tri Gam*?" Nina exclaimed.

"She is definitely *weird*!" Abby said.

Looking through the smeared coffee shop

window, they saw Jessie sitting in the booth alone, still waiting for her food. She was toying with the knife, twirling it between her fingers . . . and she had the *strangest* smile on her face.

Chapter 5

"Hi, Leila. I was hoping you'd be here."

Nina pulled off her down vest and red wool muffler and tossed them across the small, cluttered dorm room, onto her unmade bed. She leaned against the door and tried to catch her breath. "Oh. Wow. I ran all the way." She couldn't wait to tell Leila about Abby and hear Leila's opinion of the pledge meeting.

Leila stood in the middle of the room, hands on her waist, her thumbs tucked into the belt loops of her dress, glaring at Nina. She hadn't changed into more comfortable clothes, even though it was nearly two hours since the meeting had ended. "Where have you been?" she asked, sounding more like an angry parent than a roommate.

"Hey — what's wrong?" Nina asked, taking a few steps away from the door.

"Where have you been?" Leila repeated, without moving or changing her angry expression.

Uh-oh, Nina thought. She'd seen Leila angry before. She always started off quietly with clenched teeth and a cold, hard stare that could cut through steel — and then she'd explode. Nina could never figure out why Leila thought she had the right to get so furious at her friends. Maybe it was because she was an only child and never really had to control her temper, Nina thought.

She lifted a stack of books off the room's only armchair and sat down, preparing herself for the explosion to come. "I — I went for coffee with Abby," she said, trying to stare back at Leila, but looking down at the brown shag rug instead.

"That figures," Leila said, moving her thumbs furiously back and forth through the wide belt loops at her sides.

"What do you mean?" Nina cried, trying not to sound whiny and upset. "What are you bent out of shape about?"

"It figures that you'd go out for coffee with my biggest enemy in the world."

"*Enemy?*" Despite her attempts to keep it down, Nina's voice rose several octaves. "Leila — what happened between you and Abby . . . that was at least a year ago. I'm sure Abby has forgotten all — "

"No one has forgotten anything!" Leila said. Now there was more sadness than anger in her voice. Tears formed in her eyes. She shook her head hard, as if trying to shake away her feelings.

"She hates me!" Leila cried. "Abby hates me — and I don't blame her. I have Gordon and she doesn't. Don't you remember *any-thing*, Nina? Doesn't anything ever penetrate that little-girl world you live in? Abby was so upset when Gordon — when Gordon decided he liked me better — her mother had to take her out of school for nearly a year. She told everyone that Abby had gone to live with her grandmother for a while."

"I remember," Nina said quietly, her eyes still on the small brown rug. "It was a long time ago. Abby's okay now. Really. She's — "

"*I* haven't forgotten!" Leila screamed. "Believe me — Abby hasn't either!"

"I just had coffee with her. I didn't — " Nina hated herself for sounding so apologetic. She had every right to have coffee with anyone she wanted to! Struggling to control her anger, she squeezed the worn arms of the chair until her knuckles turned white. "Leila, you can't be angry because I had a cup of coffee with Abby. What's *really* bugging you?"

Nina expected the question to catch Leila off-guard, to interrupt her fury for just a second. But it only seemed to make Leila angrier.

She raised a hand up, tossed her long braid behind her shoulder, and swung around. She took three quick steps to her dresser, picked up a small, brown leather case, and tossed it as hard as she could at Nina. "Here — I got you a present!"

"Hey! Don't!" Nina cried, ducking away.

The case hit the arm of Nina's chair and bounced onto the rug at her feet.

"Go ahead. Pick it up," Leila challenged from across the room.

Nina leaned forward and reached for it, keeping her eyes on her roommate. "What is it?"

"The perfect gift for you. Binoculars."

Nina dropped the case as if it were hot and sat back in the chair. "What's *with* you, Leila? What are you *talking* about?"

Leila's beautiful heart-shaped mouth curled into a sneer. "They're for spying, Nina. Perfect for you. The next time you want to spy on Gordon and me, you'll get a much better view!" Leila glared at Nina. "I'm hurt, Nina," she said. "I'm so hurt."

Nina felt a stab of pain behind her eyes. So Leila had seen her in the parking lot. "Listen, Leila — I wasn't spying. I was walking back to the room. I couldn't help it if — "

"If what?" Leila demanded. "If you stopped and watched us for twenty minutes?!"

"I did *not*!" Nina screamed. She could feel herself losing control now — and she didn't care. "Why were you in the parking lot, Leila? What were you trying to do? You're so crazy about Gordon you don't care what happens to you — you don't care about *anything*?"

"You're jealous. That's it." Since Nina was the one screaming now, Leila lowered her voice to an angry whisper. "You're just jealous. Why don't you admit it? You've never even had a boyfriend — *have* you? *Have* you?!"

The stab of pain behind her eyes had become a full-fledged headache. Nina rubbed her eyes, tried to rub away the pain. "I — I don't have to answer that."

"You don't have to do anything," Leila said, her voice still a shuddering whisper. She grabbed her fur coat off her bed with a violent sweep of her hand and started quickly toward the door. "But one of us has to leave. I'm not rooming with a spy. An enemy!"

"Leila — stop. Just stop. This is ridiculous! We have to talk this out."

"There's nothing more to say," Leila said. She slammed the door behind her.

For a long time after Leila left, Nina sat in the armchair, staring down at the binocular case, trying to rub away her headache.

This just wasn't fair, she thought.

How could Leila *do* this to her?

She had looked forward to this night for so long. The first pledge meeting of the Tri Gams, and two of her oldest friends were there with her. It should have been exciting. It should have been fun.

She buried her head in her arm and fought to keep back the tears.

Why didn't *anything* ever work out the way she imagined it would?

The front door clicked quietly as Abby

closed it behind her and stepped into the living room. The house was dark and silent.

She stood by the door for a long while, smiling and listening to the silence. She was relieved that her mother had gone to bed. She didn't really feel like telling her about the meeting or about seeing Nina and Leila.

The air was thick and pungently sweet. Abby remembered a vase of wilting flowers on the coffee table she had forgotten to toss out. The scent was bringing back a memory. Where was it? Where was she when she had smelled that same decaying flower smell?

"What are you smiling about?"

The loud voice, so close to her, made Abby cry out.

"Gabriella — I didn't know you were. . . . Why are you sitting in the dark?"

Gabriella laughed. She enjoyed startling her sister. "I like the dark."

"It's pitch black in here," Abby said, her heart still pounding. "How can you see me smiling?"

"I know you," Gabriella said mysteriously.

"Well, don't sneak up on me like that," Abby said angrily.

Gabriella laughed again, a deep, throaty laugh. "Tell me about the meeting."

"Why? So you can make fun of it?" Abby had no patience for Gabriella. She just wanted to go up to her room, lie down on her bed, and sift through her thoughts. She needed to figure out how she felt about everything that had happened, to put everything in order in her mind.

"Me? Make fun of *you*?" Gabriella said innocently.

"Really, Gabriella — I'm in no mood for your sarcasm," Abby said, keeping her voice down so she wouldn't wake her mother. "And I don't want to fight with you."

"Me either," Gabriella said. She reached to turn on a lamp.

"Don't turn that on. I'm going right to bed," Abby told her.

"Come on. Tell me everything."

"No. Stop." Abby started toward the stairs.

"Then just tell me *one* thing," Gabriella said.

"Gabriella, please — " Why was her sister always such a pest?

"Just tell me what you think about the crime," Gabriella said, suddenly whispering. "Are you going to do it? Do you think it's for real?"

"Good night," Abby said, ignoring the questions. "And don't follow me." She began running quickly up the stairs.

She stopped near the top landing.

How did Gabriella know about the crime?

She wasn't at the meeting. *How did she know?*

Abby didn't have a chance to find out the answer. She climbed the rest of the stairs, flicked on the light in her room, and found someone waiting for her there.

Chapter 6

"Gordon! What are you *doing* here?"

Abby's voice came out tiny and choked. She looked shocked enough to scream. Gordon lifted himself off her bed quickly, stepped forward, and clamped a hand gently over her mouth. His hand felt rough and hot.

"Shhhh, Abby. Don't scream," he whispered. Then, slowly, he removed his hand.

For an instant, she realized she wanted him to keep it there. She took a step back. "Gordon, I don't *believe* this!"

"Shhhhh." He grinned at her, his face inches from hers.

She took another step back, turned, and closed the bedroom door.

"How did you get in?"

Still grinning, he pointed to the window. "Climbed," he said. Then he shrugged.

She stared at him, trying to make sure it was really him, not a look-alike, not a ghost, not a daydream figure come to life, a figure sprung from her over-active imagination.

But Gordon was too big to be an illusion. He was tall, over six feet, and muscular, built like a football player, although he never played.

His jeans were faded and torn at one knee. His sweat shirt had a grease stain down the left sleeve. It looked as if he'd been wearing it for weeks.

Gordon's brown hair was long and fell in unwashed disarray nearly to his shoulders. Patches of dark stubble dotted his jutting jaw. His narrow blue eyes, set a bit too close to his nose, still seemed to be mocking everything they saw.

He still looks like Sean Penn, Abby decided. Like a big, unwashed Sean Penn.

As she stared at him, he seemed to lose confidence. His grin faded. He shoved his big hands into his jeans pockets. He glanced back at the window from which he had entered, as if maybe he was thinking about leaving.

"How long have you been here?" Abby whispered.

"A while."

"How did you know I. . . . What made you think. . . ."

"Leila," he said, looking at the window again.

He never was much of a talker, Abby remembered. But these one-word answers were driving her bananas! "Well — what do you want?" she asked impatiently.

Her sharpness seemed to hurt him. He shrugged again. It was his turn to stare at her. "I had to explain."

She waited for him to go on, but he didn't. Looking at him in the shadowy light from the small lamp on her bedtable, she felt all mixed up. Attracted to him. Repelled by him. Frightened of him.

If only he would *talk*!

"Gordon — you had to explain *what*?"

He picked up a lipstick on her dressing table and then put it back without looking at it. "You know. I felt bad."

"You came to apologize to me?"

He picked up the lipstick again and began twirling it between his long fingers. "Well, yeah. I guess. Explain. Apologize. You know."

Abby angrily grabbed the lipstick from his hand and slammed it onto the tabletop. "There's nothing to explain, Gordon. Go home. Okay?"

His eyes went back to the window. "Come on, Abby. I'll go in a second. I — I don't know. Last year, I was just immature, I guess. I mean . . . I wasn't ready. I didn't mean to hurt you or anything."

"Well, you *did* hurt me. A lot."

She surprised herself with this bitter reply. Surprised and frightened herself. There were feelings she'd long held deep down that she wanted to *keep* deep down.

"I know. That's why I came to apologize."

Gordon's voice trembled. She'd never heard him sound so . . . real.

Her mind flashed suddenly on the night he had burned his foot. She pictured the bonfire, the kids in their down coats, mufflers, bright woolly gloves, their faces glowing orange and red, reflecting the blazing, crackling fire, the cheerleaders, the happy voices, the chants and cheers echoing off the stadium wall.

Was it homecoming or just a big pep rally? No. It was homecoming that Gordon had decided to pull his goofy, stupid stunt.

She could see him clearly. She was standing so close to the fire when he did it. She saw him take a running start, heard him screaming "GERONIMO!" at the top of his lungs, saw his wild face, his crazy eyes — and realized at once that he planned to leap over the fire.

"STOP HIM!" she had yelled.

But no one could hear her over the cheering, the laughter, the happy shouts.

"GERONIMO!"

She saw him leap. Heard gasps of surprise. Then . . . gasps of horror. His shoe. His shoe was on fire.

Crazy fool.

Crazy Gordon.

He rolled on the stadium grass. They stomped it out. They found a tarp to cover him. It must have hurt like crazy. But Crazy Gordon never let on.

He never cried out. He never uttered a word.

It was unreal.

Crazy macho Gordon couldn't let on that he was in pain.

He had a little bit of a limp now. But the foot was okay. If it hurt him, he still never let on.

Why was Abby remembering all this?

Because *now* he was letting on. Now he was being . . . real.

"Anyway . . ." he said, his voice still unsteady. "That's all, I guess. . . ."

She took a step toward him, then another. She threw her arms around his neck and pushed her lips, burning lips, against his.

Am I really doing this? she thought.

And then she stopped thinking.

She closed her eyes and kissed him harder, again, again, tightening her arms around his neck.

Gordon stepped back, tried to pull away. But soon he was returning her kiss.

Oh . . . oh . . . oh . . . she told herself. . . . If Leila ever finds out, she'll *kill* me!

Chapter 7

The house, set back in the woods at the end of the Dune Road, could have been the setting for *The Amityville Horror* or some other horror movie. The bus bumped up the rutted dirt driveway past gnarled, old trees that shivered and entwined around each other as if they were afraid of the dark.

The headlights cut through the thick fog, providing the only light. From her window seat, Abby could see a shadowy carpet of leaves on the ground, shifting, rolling, separating as if invisible creatures were running over them. Her first glimpse of the house, so dark, so rambling and rundown, so eerily perched on the desolate, forested dune, gave her a growing feeling of dread.

"Couldn't we stay at the Holiday Inn?" Jessie called from the back of the bus.

A few girls laughed — short, nervous laughs. But most of them had already learned to ignore Jessie's loud remarks and odd attempts at humor.

The engine whined as the bus began to climb the final, steep incline that curved up to the front of the house. Abby held her watch up close to her face and struggled to steady it and read it in the dark. Ten-fifteen.

The ride from the Tri Gam house had seemed really long, partly because of heavy traffic on the expressway, partly because of Jessie's insistence on trying to make funny comments about everything they passed, and partly because of the uncertainty of where they were going and what they were about to do.

"Come on, people. It's time to prove that you're Tri Gams," was all Andrea had said back on the campus as she ushered them up onto the old, yellow mini-bus. They'd had no idea they'd be heading out to the ocean — and to this deserted wreck of a mansion so far from town, so far from *anything*.

But the uncertainty of their destination wasn't the only cause of tension on the bus. Abby saw immediately that Nina and Leila weren't speaking to each other. Upon boarding, Leila had flashed Nina a real look of hate, a look so intense, it actually made Abby turn her head away.

I hope no one ever looks at *me* that way, Abby told herself. Then she remembered Gordon that night in her room — was it a week ago already? — his kisses, and between the kisses, his words of apology, of regret. If

Leila only knew . . ." Abby said to herself, she would hate me, too. . . .

But what were Leila and Nina fighting about? Probably some silly squabble about their dorm room, Abby thought. She couldn't picture the two of them living together at all. Leila was so tidy and neat, so together, so cool and sophisticated. And Nina was always such a slob, such a . . . kid.

As they boarded the rented mini-schoolbus, Leila walked past Nina, flashed Abby a quick, phony smile, and kept walking down the narrow aisle, taking a seat near the back. Rebecca climbed in beside Nina. The two of them began chattering and laughing, their high, scratchy voices reminding Abby of those cartoon chipmunks on TV.

A girl named Emily introduced herself and took the seat beside Abby. She was quite pretty in an ordinary, everyday pretty kind of way. She seemed gung-ho about everything — loved Rockland State, loved the Tri Gams, loved her courses, loved the other pledges, loved the North Shore, loved the idea of going off somewhere to commit a crime. She thought it was all a lark, just a fun sorority prank — and she loved the whole idea.

Abby tried to keep a conversation going with Emily. But it was hard to keep up the level of enthusiasm it took to talk to such a tirelessly cheerful person. The silences became longer and more awkward, and soon both girls gave up and stared out the bus window, watching the fog settle on the sides of the expressway.

A lot of the girls were finding it difficult to make conversation. It was hard to keep the purpose of the trip from their minds. They weren't off on a fun vacation trip, a weekend frolic. Before the weekend was out, they were supposed to commit a crime, a serious crime, according to Andrea, who would be accompanying them, watching them, not only an accomplice but a judge.

Three girls had refused to come along, had simply given up their chances of becoming Tri Gams. Most of the remaining seven, judging from the conversations Abby overheard on the bus, believed the whole thing to be a goof, a joke they had to play along with to prove they were good sports. Only Jessie (of course!) seemed excited about actually having the chance to commit a crime!

How did Abby feel about it? She tried to sort out her thoughts as the bus rumbled along the expressway, but she couldn't come to any decision.

She felt ... uncomfortable.

That was all.

They were nearing the end of the expressway, the final exit, where they would turn onto the local road that led to the Dune Road, when the bus suddenly squealed to a stop. Traffic normally wasn't heavy this far out of town. What could be tying things up?

Staring through the billowing fog, Abby could make out a car on the side of the road. Its headlights were on high-beam. Its doors had been flung open. The two occupants of the car, a large man in a bulky tan overcoat and a young boy, were in front of the car, in the glare of the white headlights, and they were hunched over what appeared to be a huge brown sack.

No. Wait. It wasn't a sack they were examining. Abby stared harder. It was an animal. A deer.

"Oh no! It's dead! They killed it!" Abby heard Nina cry out.

A few other girls uttered cries of surprise and revulsion.

The deer must have run out onto the highway, and the car had struck it. Now it lay on its side, unmoving, a dead heap, nothing but a big, brown sack. The man and the boy were walking around it now, still hunched over, shaking their heads.

"Oh, look — a Deer Crossing sign right next to it!" Jessie called out. "Isn't that *ironic*?"

"Jessie — *really*!" Andrea called from her seat beside the bus driver.

No one else said anything. The traffic began to move again. The bus jerked forward, backfired, jerked again, and then began to move away.

Abby kept picturing this innocent creature

taking a quick, clean leap onto the highway
... and then THUD.

She felt worse than uncomfortable now.

This is where her feelings of dread began,
long before she saw the spooky old mansion
on the dune. Again and again she saw the
innocent creature ... the leap ... the hit. ...

The girls on this bus are all innocent creatures, too, she told herself. Hey, Abby — such
weird thoughts. Don't lose control, girl. Got
to get control. ...

She forced herself to stop thinking about it.
Think about Gordon instead. She could change
her thoughts, but she couldn't rid herself of
the feeling that crept up from the pit of her
stomach, that tightened the muscles in the
back of her neck, that made her shiver even
though it was hot and steamy inside the bus.

Now the long, uncomfortable ride was over
and they were inside the old mansion. "Close
the door. Don't let the cold in," Andrea yelled.
She flicked a row of switches, and the whole
house seemed to light up.

Abby smiled, happy to be out of the darkness. The house wasn't as bad as the outside
had led them to believe. It was well lit and
cheerfully decorated with surprisingly modern, comfortable-looking furniture. And it
was warm and dry.

She took a few steps into the living room
and looked beyond it to a long dining room.
Not bad, she thought. No broken windows, no
creaking floorboards, no bats, or creepy-

looking housekeepers appearing out of nowhere.

Maybe this won't be a horror show, after
all, Abby thought, unsnapping her down
jacket. If the Tri Gams were going to take
you out to a deserted mansion to commit a
crime, at least they did it in style and comfort.

"Okay, people." Andrea herded everyone
into the big living room. "I have the room
assignments here." She pulled a yellow sheet
of paper from her coat pocket. "The driver
will bring in your bags. Your rooms are all
upstairs. I think you can find them yourselves."

She began to read her list. Nina and Rebecca were rooming together. Emily and a
very quiet girl named Ruby were roommates
for the night.

Abby felt the dread returning. What if . . .

"Leila and Abby in Room 212," Andrea
said.

It had happened. She and Leila. No. Should
she say something?

But what?

What excuse could she give for not wanting
to room with Leila?

She glanced over at Leila, who smiled back
at her, a warm smile that seemed almost
genuine.

Oh well. It's just for a night or two.

They could just avoid talking about anything . . . real.

It wouldn't be so bad.

She smiled back at Leila.

"Wait just a daggone minute here!" someone was yelling. Who would talk like that? Abby looked around. Oh. It was Jessie.

"Wait a daggone minute," Jessie repeated. "I need my privacy."

"What? What do you mean?" Andrea tried not to sound exasperated, but she couldn't help it.

"I need my own room. To myself," Jessie said, as if Andrea should have understood it from the beginning.

There were giggles and whispered remarks around the big living room, all of them at Jessie's expense. Andrea stared at her list. "Okay, Jessie. Room 233 is empty because Charlotte and Ruth decided not to join us. You can have that room."

"Good," Jessie said, as if an injustice had been righted.

"Get some sleep, guys," Andrea said, folding up the list and jamming it back into her coat pocket. "Tomorrow we have some important scouting to do."

The girls all headed toward the stairway. Leila, still smiling warmly, leaned against the mahogany bannister and waited for Abby.

Abby tried to smile back, but her mouth wouldn't cooperate. "Hi, Leila. I guess we — "

"I hope you don't plan to have a long chat tonight," Leila said, covering a yawn with her hand. Abby couldn't help but notice her perfect, long, blood-red fingernails. "I'm totally wrecked."

"No, I — I mean . . . so am I." Abby hoped she didn't sound too grateful.

"Maybe we can catch up on each other's lives tomorrow," Leila said, actually sounding friendly. "I just can't keep my eyes open. I guess it was the bus ride. I don't know."

"Fine. Great!" Abby said, feeling a little silly.

She followed Leila up the long staircase to their room. This trip has already had one surprise, Abby thought. Leila was nice to me.

A few minutes later, she fell asleep wondering what other surprises were in store.

In the summertime, vacationers and summer people filled the narrow main street of the little town, trying on bathing suits and chic summer gear in the trendy boutiques with names like SEE-WORTHY and DUNE-FINE, buying backyard furniture, pastel shaded posters, and barbecue grilles for their summer houses, and lunching on shrimp salad and pasta in the outdoor cafes and small restaurants.

But in the fall, the streets were nearly empty, the summer people had packed up their bikes and tennis gear and gone home, and most of the stores were closed and boarded up.

"It's so empty. It's almost like a movie

set," Leila said to Abby as they crossed the car less street. Leila was being super friendly to Abby. Abby was relieved. Leila's easygoing chit-chat, as if the two of them were the best of friends, as if nothing had happened between them, was making the weekend a lot easier.

"Look at those dogs," Abby said, laughing. Two scraggly, black mutts were lying on their backs in the middle of Main Street, looking as if they owned the town.

"Try to keep up," Andrea called from up ahead. The girls obediently quickened their pace.

Andrea had had the driver park the bus at the big lot at the edge of town near the railroad tracks, even though there were parking places all up and down Main Street.

"I want to walk you through town so you can memorize where everything is," she had said, sounding very serious and businesslike. "Memorize everything. Your life may depend on it."

"Look out!" cried Jessie, as she stepped off the bus. "We're bad. We're *baaad*! Here comes the Gamma Gamma Gamma Gang!"

Andrea just rolled her eyes and motioned for everyone to follow. They walked past Del's Deli and The Old-Fashioned New Fashion Store, both boarded up. A strong wind blew through the street, carrying a cold and wet chill from the ocean nearby.

A boy of about ten or eleven in just jeans

and a T-shirt came speeding by on a beat-up racing bike. "Hey — don't you need a coat?" Jessie yelled after him.

"I'm not cold!" the boy cried without slowing down or looking back.

Everyone laughed. Nervous laughter.

At the far end of the street, Andrea stopped in front of a large store with a bulky, solid oak coffee table in the window. "Here we are," she said, smiling and pointing to the hand-painted sign above the door: DRIFTWOOD ANTIQUES.

A sign taped to the glass door said OPEN. Andrea pulled open the door and motioned everyone inside.

The store was quite large, but there was little room to walk around. It was filled with antique furninture of all description: huge cabinets and wardrobes, hand-carved desks, dining room tables — solid-looking furniture of rich wood, all of which appeared to weigh at least a ton. Andrea made her way past a crushed velvet Victorian sofa to the far wall. There, several glass display cases offered an array of antique jewelry.

Abby and Leila looked at each other. "You're right. This *has* to be a movie set. It can't be real," Abby said.

Lelia ran her hand over the surface of a round cocktail table sculpted of dappled marble. "Just the kind of light, breezy furniture to put in your summer home," she said sarcastically.

"Hey — anyone home?" Jessie called. "There's no one minding the store."

"Jessie, please — " Andrea started.

But the store owner stepped out from a tiny back office. She was a small, elderly woman, her white hair tight in a bun, wearing an attractive violet suit. She was carrying some sort of ledger book, which she dropped in surprise when she saw that her store was filled with young women.

"Oh my — I didn't know. . . ." She had a surprisingly young voice for someone who looked to be at least sixty-five or seventy.

Andrea bent down quickly and picked up the book for her.

"Thank you. I didn't expect. . . . I wasn't even going to open up today. There are so few people around." She set the ledger down on the marble cocktail table.

"We're cheerleaders. We're on a bus trip from our college in Pennsylvania," Andrea told her. It was a well-rehearsed lie. It sounded completely true.

"How nice," the woman said, her smile revealing lipstick-stained teeth. "I'm Marie Driftwood. Yes. That's really my name. I'm the only Driftwood you'll find in this store. Ha ha!" She had a little girl laugh.

"Well, it's a beautiful store," Andrea said. "We were all admiring the jewelry."

Mrs. Driftwood started to say something, but the phone in the back office suddenly rang. "Oh, excuse me. Look around, girls. I'll be right back." She began scurrying through the maze of tables and sofas to get to the back office. "Coming. I'm coming!"

Andrea smiled after her until she disappeared into the back office. Then her earnest, businesslike expression immediately returned. "There's the side entrance," she said quietly, pointing. "And there's the cash register. Memorize everything. *Everything*."

"We're doing our crime here?" Nina cried, in a high, little voice.

"That's right, Nina," Andrea said. Her usually colorless eyes seemed to light up at the thought. "Tomorrow, we're coming back here for the jewels you see in those cases, and for all the money in the cash register."

"But — " Nina started.

"Not another word," Andrea said quietly, her eyes still blazing. "You can talk at the meeting tonight . . . when we decide who gets to carry the gun."

Chapter 8

"Wow. It's a lot like old times, isn't it?" Nina said. But the jump of her voice made it more of a question than a statement. "You and Leila seem to be getting along fine."

Abby put the old copy of *Glamour* down on her lap, raised her arms above her head, and stretched. "Yeah. Isn't that weird?"

"Uh-huh," Nina agreed. "It's weird, I guess."

Two other girls, Emily and the girl named Ruby, who was dark and exotic, the exact opposite of Emily, wandered into the living room and settled onto a red leather loveseat near the flickering light of the fireplace. Abby couldn't help but smile. Ruby appeared to be having difficulty keeping a conversation going with Emily, too.

"Well, be careful, Abby," Nina continued.

"What?" Watching the girls across the room, Abby had lost the thread of the conversation. "About what?"

"About Leila. Don't trust her." Nina's freckled face tightened into a concerned frown.

Nina looks so funny when she tries to be serious, Abby thought. "You two have a fight or something?" Abby asked her, a bit too loudly.

Emily looked away from the fireplace and gave Abby a little wave. Rebecca entered the room, looking even taller than usual in tight, green, straight-legged jeans. She was wearing a Walkman and walking in time to the music she was hearing. Snapping her fingers loudly, she settled down on the rug in front of the fire, a long, green grasshopper.

"Yeah," Nina said, still frowning. "You know Leila. She can really blow up."

"She'll get over it," Abby told her, seeing that Nina was really upset about it.

"I don't think so," Nina said. "I don't think Leila gets over things, Abby. I know I'm not being too subtle or anything — but don't trust her. Don't think she really wants to be your friend again just because she's being nice — "

Something about Abby's eyes made Nina stop talking. Nina looked away, broke the connection.

Abby saw Leila enter the room, looking stunning in jeans and a plain gray sweatshirt, her gleaming hair unbraided, falling carelessly around her face. Leila looked around the room, didn't seem to see Abby and

Nina — or pretended not to see them — and then walked quickly toward Emily and Ruby to claim the armchair across from them. The armchair seat cushion was deep and soft, and as Leila sank down, it looked as if she were being swallowed whole by the chair.

That made Nina laugh. Leila, struggling to pull herself up to a comfortable position, glared straight ahead at the fire, pretending not to hear Nina's giggle.

"What's so funny?" Abby asked.

Nina turned back to her. She was relieved to see that Abby's eyes had returned to normal. "Nothing," Nina told her.

"What did you and Leila fight about — " Abby asked. " — Which of you left a hair on her comb?"

Nina giggled again. She liked it when people said sarcastic things. She never knew how to be sarcastic herself. "Oh, what's the point," she said, shrugging her small shoulders. "Remember I told you about her and Gordon in the parking lot? Well . . . she thinks I was spying on them."

Gordon. The word sent a flash of warmth to Abby's cheeks. Was she blushing? She pictured Gordon waiting for her in her bedroom. Kissing her. Again.

"Yeah. You're right," Abby said aloud.

"What?" Nina was confused.

"Oh, sorry," Abby said, shaking her head. "I was thinking of something else."

Nina *was* right. Leila could never be her friend again.

"Okay, people. It's eight o'clock. Are we ready for our meeting?" Andrea burst into the room, walking at her usual full speed, as chipper as ever. You'd think she had come to organize a bake sale or to start rehearsals on a school play instead of to plan an armed holdup.

She walked quickly up to the front of the room and stood with her back to the fire. "Everyone comfortable?" She surveyed the room, smiling brightly. The fire seemed to radiate around her. For a moment it looked to Abby as if Andrea was the source of the fire. Then it looked as if Andrea had been consumed by the darting, dancing flames. Her form became shadowy and indistinct. She seemed to flicker and fold with the flames.

Abby closed her eyes. When she opened them, Andrea had moved to the side of the fireplace. "Hey — where's Jessie?" she asked, looking at her watch.

"Haven't seen her," Rebecca's little mouse voice called.

"Anybody see her?" Andrea asked.

"Here I am," Jessie called from the entranceway. "I guess my watch stopped." She held up her bare arm. "It still says three hairs past six. Ha ha!"

No one laughed. "Jessie — please try to be on time," Andrea scolded. "It won't do to-

morrow if someone is late. Our timing must
be perfect."

"Is there any other soap we can use?"
Jessie asked. "The soap in the bathroom is
too harsh. It hurts my skin."

"Jes-sie," Andrea groaned, sounding really
out of patience. "We're not talking about
soap now. We're talking about tomorrow. It's
really important that we all know the plan
and know what we're doing. And if you want
to talk about soap —"

"What if we screw up tomorrow?" Leila
asked suddenly.

The question — from a new voice —
seemed to confuse Andrea. But only for a
moment. She turned to Leila, who had draped
one leg up over the arm of the big armchair,
and took a few steps toward her.

"We don't screw up," Andrea said flatly.
The phrase seemed odd coming from her perfect little mouth. She raised herself up on tiptoe, then quickly came back down. "No group
of Tri Gamma pledges has ever screwed up.
No one has ever been caught. No crime has
ever been solved."

She started to go back to her place beside
the fire, but Leila wasn't finished. "A lot of
us think this is all a joke," she said. It was a
nervy thing to say, something all of the girls
in the big living room wanted to hear said.

"Then a lot of you will be in for a big surprise," Andrea replied, looking around the
room.

"But you don't really mean —" Leila started.

Andrea held up a hand to stop her in mid-sentence. "Being accepted into this sorority isn't a joke," she said, pronouncing each word slowly and carefully. "The traditions of the Tri Gams are old, and tested, and true. Also not a joke. When we say we want to bind you to us, to make you Tri Gams for life — that isn't a joke. And — and —"

She walked quickly up to a tall cabinet against the wall, removed a key from around her neck, and unlocked a small compartment in the base of the cabinet. "Here!" Andrea cried triumphantly.

She held up a silver pistol. It seemed to shimmer and flame in the firelight. "This isn't a joke, either, Leila," she said, holding the pistol tightly in her hand, raising it high so everyone could see it. "It's real. It's very real. And one of you lucky girls will soon find out how real it is."

Up on tiptoes again, Andrea placed the pistol down carefully on the tall mantelpiece. When she turned back to face everyone, her calm and her smile had returned. "Are there any other questions?"

Silence.

"Can we talk about the soap later?" Jessie asked from the back of the room.

This time, everyone laughed.

Jessie was certainly great for breaking the tension.

But Andrea didn't seem to want the tension broken. She ignored Jessie and launched into the plan for the holdup.

At first Abby found it amusing that this prim-looking, Miss Perfect sorority-girl type would be talking so glibly about putting fake license plates on the bus, catching the store-owner off-guard, subduing and tying her up, assigning lookouts for the two doors, and using separate escape routes if anyone should intrude. But Andrea seemed so involved, so carried away by it all, so *high* from it, Abby's amusement soon turned to disgust.

Despite Andrea's heated assurances, Abby still believed the whole thing was a joke. But the way Andrea was handling it, in Abby's opinion, had turned it into a very nasty joke, a completely unpleasant and upsetting experience. And what was the point of that?

"Okay. Everyone draws a straw," Andrea said, holding up the dark-colored straws the way she held the pistol. "Short straw carries the pistol."

She stepped up to Ruby and pushed her closed fist of straws toward her. "No," Ruby said, shaking her head, long, dangling earrings shaking with her.

"Take a straw," Andrea insisted.

"No," Ruby said quietly. "I won't. I mean, I'm not. I'm not going to do it."

"You're not going to join us tomorrow?" Andrea sounded more hurt than surprised.

"No," Ruby said, more determined with each refusal. She stared back at Andrea. "No. I'm not coming. It's . . . I think it's stupid. The whole thing."

Andrea took a step back, without lowering the fistful of straws. "But, Ruby — come on. You can't be accepted . . . you can't be a Tri Gam unless you join us."

"I know," Ruby said, quickly getting up. "I'm sorry. I just don't want to. I can't. Sorry. I'll just — I'll call my friend to come pick me up tonight."

"No," Andrea said, looking toward the fire. "You can't do that."

"Why not?" Ruby cried, suddenly sounding a little afraid.

"There's no phone," Andrea said, offering her the straws one more time.

"No," Ruby said, standing awkwardly just a few inches from Andrea. "Sorry."

"I'm sorry, too," Andrea said, giving Ruby an odd half-smile. "You'll have to wait here at the house till it's time to leave. You don't want to come to town with us, and there are no houses near enough to walk to."

"Well . . . okay," Ruby said uncertainly. "I'll wait here."

"What about the cops?" Jessie asked loudly. "Do you have a plan for dealing with them, Andrea?"

Andrea held the straws in front of Rebecca, who quickly reached up from her place on the rug and pulled out — a long one. Rebbeca laughed giddily and tossed the straw into the fire.

"The police pretty much close down at the end of summer, too," Andrea said, moving on to Emily. "There may be a few on duty. But they'll probably be out on highway detail. They're pretty old and fat. They're no sweat."

Without thinking, Abby laughed out loud. It just struck her funny that Andrea in her crewneck Esprit sweater and pleated skirt would be trying to talk so tough. Nina gave Abby an odd look, but no one else seemed to notice.

Everyone was concentrating on Andrea's fist and the remaining straws. Leila pulled a long one. Jessie, holding one hand over her eyes as a blindfold and starting to pull first one, changing her mind, trying another, then a third, pulled a long one.

"Your turn, Nina," Andrea said, grinning.

Abby felt her heart begin to pound. She was next. She was last. If Nina pulled a long straw, that meant . . . that meant. . . .

Nina pulled the short straw.

She screamed at the top of her lungs, the little stub of a straw flying out of her hand. "No! No!"

Andrea laughed.

She sure is enjoying this, Abby thought, breathing a sigh of relief. Poor Nina.

"Well, well, Nina. I guess *you* don't think this is all a joke — *do* you!" Andrea exclaimed happily. She walked over to the mantel, went up on tiptoe to retrieve the pistol, and delivered it to Nina.

Nina couldn't decide whether to hold it by the handle or the barrel. "It — it's real . . ." she said weakly, staring at it as if it were some kind of creature that had dropped down from outer space.

"Careful. It's loaded," Andrea said, a pleased grin crossing her face.

Nina didn't say anything. She looked at Abby, who looked at Andrea.

"If all goes well tomorrow morning," Andrea said ominously, "you won't have to use it, Nina." She paused for dramatic effect. "I hope you won't have to use it. Mrs. Driftwood seems like such a nice old lady. . . ."

"Ruby's the only one with any guts here," Leila said disgustedly. She sat down gracefully on top of the heavy maroon bedspread and stretched.

"Andrea would say that Ruby is the only coward," Abby said, flopping down in the wooden chair by the desk.

The meeting had ended a few minutes before. The pledges were instructed to get right to bed. But who could sleep?

Leila and Abby found themselves talking at the same time, agreeing that it was all a big joke. But they didn't agree on much else.

"It's not worth it," Leila declared, lying on her back, staring up at the gold and chrome light fixture that dangled from the ceiling on a long brass chain. "Why put yourself through all this craziness?"

"It's worth it," Abby said, more vehemently than she had intended. "Sure, it's a drag. But it's worth it. To be a Tri Gam? To be the best?"

Leila started to say something but, looking at Abby's expression, thought better of it. "It means a lot to you to get in, huh?"

Before Abby could answer, they both heard a loud rapping on the window pane.

At first they thought it must be a tree limb battering against the glass. But a second rapping with a definite rhythm revealed that someone was at the window.

As the girls stared, frightened, trying to decide whether or not to run from the room, the window opened quickly and two black boots, followed by two blue-jeaned legs, slid down into the room.

"Gordon!" Abby cried.

Grinning triumphantly, a denim motorcycle cap pulled at a slashing angle down across his forehead, Gordon hopped into the room.

"You're here!" Abby cried happily, raising her arms and rushing toward him.

But Gordon, grinning even broader through his two-day stubble, stepped quickly past Abby and pulled Leila up from the bed in a big embrace.

Feeling her face grow bright red and hot,

Abby turned around. Leila was staring at her over Gordon's shoulder, giving her the oddest look, surprise and suspicion mixed with utter contempt.

"Gordon! Stop! What are you *doing* here?!" Leila cried.

"I . . . uh . . . followed you. I *had* to!" Gordon declared.

I just want to sink between the floorboards and disappear, Abby thought, trembling all over from embarrassment, from disappointment, from shame. I just want to die.

Chapter 9

Nina sat hunched over the table in the break-fast room, her eyes half closed, her hair un-brushed. She looked down at her bowl of cereal, rapidly getting soggy, and made a face. "Who can think about breakfast this morning?" she said, her voice even raspier than usual.

Abby, nearly as pale as the white linen tablecloth, pointed down the table at Jessie, who had finished her second bowl of corn flakes and was rapidly downing a blueberry muffin. "Jessie doesn't seem too nervous," she said, clearing her throat, trying to wake up.

"I really think we deserve a *hot* breakfast," Jessie said loudly to no one in particular.

Andrea, looking perky and ready to face the world, walked into the room just in time to hear Jessie's complaint. "You'll be more alert if you don't have a big breakfast, Jessie," she said, sounding like a tolerant mother. "You do want to be alert, don't you?"

"I'm ready," Jessie declared through a

mouthful of blueberry muffin. "Can I at least make a pot of tea? Doesn't anyone want tea?"

No one responded.

"We don't have time," Andrea said, looking at her watch. "As soon as the driver gets the Pennsylvania plates on the bus, we're leaving for town."

This information caused a flurry of nervous conversations around the long table. Most of the girls, Abby overheard, still believed the whole thing to be a big joke. But Nina had made up her mind otherwise. "It's real, isn't it?" she whispered across the table to Abby. "We're really doing it. And I'm carrying the gun."

It occurred to Abby that for once Nina didn't look like a ten-year-old. "I don't know," she told her. "I really can't decide."

Abby looked down at the yellow breakfast plate. She had torn her blueberry muffin to small shreds without realizing it.

Why did her head feel as if it weighed five-hundred pounds?

Probably because she hadn't slept that night.

She was too embarrassed, too humiliated . . . too furious. Was she furious at herself? At Gordon? At Leila? What did it matter?

She had curled up in the big, old bed, alone, wrestling with her thoughts, replaying the moment Gordon had climbed into the room again and again — until she wanted to scream, to tear her hair, to jump . . . jump out the window into his boot tracks in the mud below.

Leila had sneaked off with Gordon, somewhere down the hall. Abby heard her tiptoe back into the room a few hours later and climb into bed with her clothes on.

What did Leila think of her now? Behind the fake smiles, the phony warmth, the half-hearted attempts to be friendly, what did Leila really think? And what did that look — that horrifying look of suspicion, of hatred — mean?

Did Leila hate Abby? Was she afraid of her? Did she pity her?

No!

She *can't* pity me, Abby thought. I won't *let* her pity me!

But rushing up to greet Gordon like that, with her arms open and ready, was *pitiful!*

"Hey — Abby — what's wrong?" Nina's scratchy voice interrupted her thoughts. "You're blushing!"

"What? Am I?" Abby could feel her face getting even hotter.

"Come on — what were you daydreaming about?" Nina demanded. "Or should I say *who?*"

"No. No, I — " Abby stammered. "I just can't seem to wake up." She glanced down the table at Leila, who was forcing down a slice of dry toast. Leila was still wearing the jeans and sweatshirt she had slept in. But her face was radiant and awake, and her hair was brushed into a stylish flow of perfect waves.

Perfect. She's perfect, Abby thought.

She *thinks* she's perfect.

She thinks. . . .

Stop it, Abby. Get control. Get control right now, girl. Don't let Leila get to you. Don't slip. Don't fall. Just — get — control.

Leila smiled across the table at Abby. A conspiratorial smile. For a second, Abby thought she was daydreaming again.

Did Leila plan to pretend that nothing had happened?

Had anything happened??

Was it possible that Leila hadn't noticed? Didn't realize that Abby believed Gordon had come to see her instead of Leila?

Had Abby made up that horrifying look Leila had given her?

Had Abby made it *all* up?

Or was this Leila's way to get through the day, to get through this awful weekend smoothly — without an ugly confrontation?

Yes. That was it. Good old phony Leila. She was so cold, so cool. She could smile her way through any situation.

That was it, all right. That had to be it.

"Okay, people. Time for action." Andrea's words stopped all of the conversations in the big room. "Five minutes to go the the bathrooms. There are two downstairs you can use, too. We don't want any embarrassing bladder accidents when things get tense, do we! Ha ha!"

No one laughed.

"Everyone looks tense *already*!" Jessie said, scraping her chair loudly against the floor as she pushed away from the table.

"Jessie — wait!" Andrea cried, alarmed. "I don't believe you, Jessie. You've got to get changed."

Jessie plopped back into her chair. "What?"

Leila was the first to see the problem. Then everyone else caught on. Jessie was wearing a ROCKLAND STATE sweatshirt! Nervous laughter echoed off the high ceiling. Jessie, finally realizing what everyone was staring at, laughed too, and bounded out of the room to get changed.

A few minutes later, they stepped out into the wet mist of an autumn shore morning, raindrop-sized dew still clinging to the tall weeds that seemed to bend away from the ocean, and boarded the yellow school bus. They rode in silence, each girl lost in her own thoughts.

The fog seemed to follow them into the bus. Abby felt chilled — and alone. She stared out the water-streaked window at the gray, empty dunes. She could hear the crashing of the ocean waves, but the fog hid the water from view.

Suddenly, she was aware of a conversation

behind her, the only voices on the bus. She turned in her seat and saw that it was Andrea, demonstrating to Nina how to use the pistol. Nina looked ten again, like a little girl who was afraid to try playing with a new mechanical toy.

"It's easy," Andrea kept repeating. "You just pull this back — and then fire."

"Fire?" Nina squeaked.

Andrea laughed. "Just like on TV. But let me tell you a little secret, Nina. I suppose I should've told you before. The bullets in the gun...."

"Yes?"

"They're not real .They're blanks. They'll make a loud noise. That's all."

"So it *is* just like on TV," Nina said, sounding very relieved.

Abby turned back to the window. Of *course* the bullets were blanks. You don't use real bullets when you're playing a joke.

And that's all it was — a joke, a bad joke that would soon be over. In an hour or so, they'd all be back at the house on the dune, packing up and laughing, telling each other what a swell time they'd all had and how they hadn't believed it was real for a minute.

"I pull this back. Then I aim ... right?"

Nina sounded a lot less frightened now.

She would do just fine. Just fine. Abby realized that, like her, Nina would probably do *anything* to become a Tri Gam. To be accepted by this sorority, by these girls who were so much more sophisticated, so much *older* than her, meant everything to Nina. No one would think of her as a kid anymore. Nina would be a Tri Gam.

Yes, Nina would go through with this escapade, gun and all. And she would do just fine.

Abby shivered. Why did it have to be so cold?

The bus pulled into town and turned down Main Street. A couple of truck drivers were walking slowly out of the small lunch counter on the corner. The grocery store owner was unlocking the door to his shop. The two dogs weren't in their place in the middle of the street. Maybe they slept late on Saturdays.

The bus pulled to a stop right across the street from Driftwood Antiques. "Three minutes, people," Andrea said, standing in the aisle beside the driver. "This should take three minutes, no longer. Get in and get out."

"Where will you be? Are you coming with us?" Jessie asked.

"I'll be right outside," Andrea said. "The bus will be running, ready to leave. When you come out, come out slowly, and board the bus naturally. Rebecca — the rope?"

Rebecca stood up. She was so tall, she had to duck her head. Rebecca had been given the assignment of tying and gagging Mrs. Driftwood. She held up the rope Andrea had given her. Her lips moved, but her little voice didn't carry to the front of the bus.

"Okay, people," Andrea said, looking at each of them one by one. "I know you can do it. Remember — you're Tri Gams. And Tri Gams can do anything!"

Abby laughed out loud. Tri Gams can do anything? Even hold up little old ladies in antique stores? Andrea had gone too far with that line! How could anyone take this seriously?

"Abby — you're laughing! You okay?" Nina asked.

"Yes, I'm — " She looked at Nina. The poor girl was trembling. "Nina — come on. Lighten up. It's just a joke. Really."

Nina raised the pistol. "A joke? I don't know, Abby. This gun feels very real."

They stepped down from the bus. The air felt fresh and cold. The fog had lifted, but clouds still covered the sun.

Andrea took up her post beside the doorway, in front of the display window with the big oak coffee table. Emily, her eyes darting from side to side, held open the door, and the girls walked quietly, determinedly into the shop.

"Why, hello. Back again?" Mrs. Driftwood, wearing a bulky wine-colored cardigan over black slacks, looked up from some papers she held on a clipboard. "I didn't — "

She stopped talking when she saw Nina.

Nina, her eyes wide and her mouth set in a tight frown of concentration, raised the pistol in one hand, pulled back the hammer with the other, took three quick steps forward, and aimed the barrel of the gun right at Mrs. Driftwood's startled face.

Chapter 10

Mrs. Diftwood's mouth curled up into an odd smile, as if she didn't believe this was happening to her. Then she began to blink rapidly and her cheek started to twitch. "What . . . what on earth. . . ."

"Just stand still," Rebecca called out, her voice even higher than usual. She stepped forward uncertainly, unwinding the thick rope in her trembling hands.

"But you girls. . . ." Mrs. Driftwood started, gripping the clipboard as if it were holding her up.

"Quiet!" Jessie yelled, startling everyone. "Come on, girls. Let's break open these jewelry cases. Hurry!"

Abby's assignment was the cash register. She headed toward it but stopped halfway as she saw Nina falter.

"Wait!" Nina called out. "I — I don't think I can do this!"

Nina lowered the gun. Her knees seemed to buckle, but she caught herself before she fell, grabbing a desktop with her free hand and holding herself up. "I — I can't. . . ."

Leila laughed. "Come on, Nina. It's only a joke," she said, sounding as if she were scolding a three-year-old. She gestured to Mrs. Driftwood. "She's in on it, too. You can tell."

"What?" The color returned to Mrs. Driftwood's face. But the blinking and twitching didn't stop. "Only a joke? What kind of a joke is this?"

"Shut up! All of you!" Jessie yelled. She was very angry for some reason. Abby figured it was because the other girls were letting her down. Jessie had a fantasy of pulling off this heist like in some crime movie or TV show. And these scaredy cats were spoiling it for her. Abby smiled. Jessie had to be the most twisted girl she had ever met.

"Give me that!" Jessie yelled, and swiped the gun from Nina's hand.

Nina looked startled, then relieved.

"This is no joke," Jessie told Mrs. Driftwood, a sneer curling her lips. "So stop twitching like that and stand still. We won't hurt you unless we have to."

"That's telling her!" Leila said, and laughed again. Was she laughing from nervousness, from fear? Or did she still believe this was all a gag? Abby couldn't decide.

"Hurry! It's supposed to be three minutes!" Jessie told everyone, waving the gun a few inches from Mrs. Driftwood's face.

Abby obediently walked to the cash register and stared at the keys, trying to figure out how to open it. She heard the sound of glass breaking against the far wall. She looked up to see Emily and Rebecca smashing in the jewelry cases with fireplace tools they had picked up.

As they scurried about the cases, breaking the glass and pulling out the jewelry, they looked as if they were speeded up, like an old silent comedy movie. Everyone seemed to be moving too fast to Abby.

"Oh! Oh no!"

And suddenly everyone froze.

"Oh! Oh! It hurts!"

Mrs. Driftwood's clipboard hit the floor and bounced across the carpet as she clutched her chest with both hands.

"It hurts! My heart! I — "

Her eyes rolled up and she sank to the floor, the back of her head thudding hard against the carpet. Her hands still clutched her chest.

She didn't move.

She wasn't moving.

Nobody moved.

Jessie, the pistol still gripped tightly in her hand, bent over her. She stared into the old woman's face for a few seconds. Then she dropped to her knees and grabbed up the frail, unmoving wrist, so thin it seemed to be nothing but bone.

Jessie searched for a pulse, shook her head,

and searched some more, squeezing the arm, pulling it, squeezing it.

She sighed and placed the arm down gently on the carpet. When she looked up, Abby was the first person she saw. "She's dead," Jessie told her. "We've killed her."

Chapter 11

"This wasn't in the script. It wasn't in the script."

Andrea kept repeating those words, pacing back and forth across the living room, shaking her head, gesturing with her hands. Her normally perfect hair was in disarray. She kept pushing her hands through it until it stood up on both sides.

"It just wasn't in the script."

A fire crackled behind her, but it offered no heat. The large living room, once so comfortable and warm, seemed drafty and damp. They had switched on all of the lamps and the lights in the large chandelier too, but the room still felt dark and gloomy.

Abby sat beside Nina on the sofa across from the fireplace and tried her best to comfort her. The girls were all upset and frightened. But Nina seemed to be in really bad shape.

"We killed. her. We're murderers!" she

said, tears streaming down her flaming cheeks.

"Nina — stop," Abby said softly, awkwardly trying to put an arm around Nina's trembling shoulder. She gave up the idea, and took her hand instead, pressing it between her two hands, trying to warm it up.

Nina had wanted to go to the town police right away. She wanted to tell them the whole story.

But Andrea had stopped her out on the street in front of the store. "First we have to regroup," Andrea had said, trying to quiet them, trying to keep the bus driver from hearing what had happened. "We have to go back to the house and make a plan. This wasn't in the script."

They had reluctantly agreed to Andrea's wishes. But now, Andrea seemed too upset to think clearly. And Nina realized they were in even worse trouble for running away.

"Nina, please . . . try to calm down," Abby repeated.

"I can't. I can't. What will happen to us? What will they do to us?"

Abby struggled to come up with an answer, but she didn't have one. She was as upset as Nina, but she was better at holding in her emotions. She *had* to hold in her emotions. I have no choice, she told herself, shivering. Someone has to be the strong one. We can't *all* fall to pieces.

"I don't know what will happen," Abby

whispered. "Maybe we won't get caught."

"What? WHAT?" Nina shrieked, growing more out of control. She jerked her hand away from Abby and started to pull at her hair.

"Nina — stop! Stop right now!" Abby screamed, trying to pull Nina's hands away from her hair. "There was no one on the street in town. No one saw us get back onto the bus. We didn't pass anyone on the way back."

Nina squirmed away from Abby and buried her face in the sofa pillow. "So? So? So what?" she cried, her voice muffled by the big cushion.

"So if no one saw us, we won't get caught. No one will know," Abby said. She realized she didn't sound very convincing. She couldn't even convince herself.

"So what? So what?" Nina cried, sitting up again. Tormented by her thoughts, by the vision of Mrs. Driftwood grabbing her chest and slumping to the hard floor, by the sound of the old lady's head hitting the floor, a sound she would never forget, Nina couldn't sit still, couldn't find a comfortable position. She felt as if she wanted to leap out of her body . . . and fly away.

"We killed her! All of us! We're all murderers!"

"Not *all* of us," Ruby said quietly. "I didn't go."

"That's right," Andrea said quickly. "And I

didn't go inside with you. I really don't know what went on . . . how it all happened."

"Now, wait a minute, Andrea —" Jessie started. "You — you're in this as much as we are! Don't try to —"

"But I'm not," Andrea insisted. She seemed to be thinking hard, working out this new idea in her mind, convincing herself as she talked. "It's true. I wasn't there. I didn't see anything."

"That's not right, Andrea," Jessie said angrily. "You can't do that to us. You brought us there. You arranged the whole thing."

"Yes — you were in charge!" Emily shouted, tears welling in her eyes. "You're the leader!"

"But I didn't kill anyone," Andrea said, looking away from them, turning her gaze to the fire. "How could I? I was outside the whole time. You girls went into the store. The next thing I knew, you all came running out, telling me the owner was dead."

"No, Andrea!" Nina leaped to her feet. "No! You can't!" She looked as if she wanted to say more. But all that came out were loud sobs.

Leila quickly rushed over to Nina and put an arm around her. She seemed to forget about their fight as she spoke softly to her old friend, hugging her, trying to stop the loud sobbing.

She led Nina back to the sofa and set her down gently next to Abby. Then she turned to Andrea. "Come on, Andrea. It's time to drop it — don't you agree?"

Andrea looked confused. "Drop it? Drop what?"

"Drop the joke, Andrea," Leila said, rolling her eyes in disgust. "It's all gone too far. Look at Nina. Look how upset everyone is. Use your better judgment, Andrea. It's time to drop the joke."

Andrea's expression didn't change. She still looked as if she didn't understand what Leila meant. "Joke? What joke, Leila?"

"This whole thing," Leila said impatiently.

"Well," Andrea replied, staring hard at Leila, "if you think this is a joke, you've got a strange sense of humor."

"Is Leila right?" Rebecca asked, her voice a shrill whisper. "It's all a joke?"

Andrea shook her head sadly. "It's not," she told them. "Thinking it's a joke isn't going to make it go away. We have a horrible situation on our hands. Horrible."

Leila threw up her hands and turned away in disgust. The room was silent except for Nina's loud sobs.

Andrea began to button her coat.

"Where are you going?" Jessie asked her.

"There's no phone in this house," Andrea said, struggling with one of the buttons. "I'm going to walk to the next house to phone the police."

"THE POLICE?" two girls cried out.

"Well . . . yes," Andrea said, not looking at

any of them. Then she quickly added, "But don't get me wrong. I'm going to support you girls the best I can. And the sorority will stand behind you, too."

"But you *can't* go to the police!" Rebecca cried.

"She *has* to!" Ruby said.

"She's right. What choice do I have, Rebecca?" Andrea asked, buttoning the final coat button. "If someone has died as the result of our . . . uh . . . trip here, it's my responsibility to report it to the authorities. As an officer of the Tri Gamma sorority, I have no choice but to call them. The reputation of the sorority — "

"But what about *our* reputations?" Nina cried through her tears. "What about our *lives*?"

Andrea shrugged. "I'm sorry. I'm going now." She started to walk quickly to the front door.

"Oh no you don't!" Jessie screamed. She ran up behind Andrea, grabbed her roughly by the shoulders, and spun her around.

"Get your hands off me!" Andrea cried, swinging her arms to free herself. "*You* held the gun, Jessie! *You're* the murderer!"

Jessie held onto her. "Shut up! Shut up! You're not going anywhere," Jessie screamed, twisting Andrea's arm behind her.

"Get off! Get *off*!" Andrea screamed, struggling to get away.

"Jessie," Leila said quietly, "let her go."

For some reason, Jessie obeyed. She let go of Andrea's arms. Andrea fell to the carpet.

"We can't keep her here as a prisoner," Leila said.

"She has to call the police. She *has* to!" Ruby insisted.

"You be quiet, or — " Jessie spun around to threaten Ruby.

"Stop it, Jessie," Leila said.

"We can't let Andrea talk to the police. She's only going to tell them how she's totally innocent — how we killed the old lady, and she had nothing to do with it!" Jessie said, rolling up the sleeves of her sweatshirt as if preparing for a fight.

"But we didn't kill her! It was an accident!" Emily cried.

"An accident with Jessie holding a gun to her head!" Andrea shouted from the carpet.

"Shut up! Shut up!" Jessie yelled, and kicked at Andrea.

"If Andrea goes to phone the police, someone should go with her," Emily suggested.

"No!" Rebecca cried. "Why do we have to call the police? No one saw us in town. Let's just go home!"

"I can't allow that," Andrea said, climbing to her feet. She began to brush the dust off her coat.

"Don't tell us what you can and cannot allow!" Jessie cried. Anger had turned her round face bright red. She looked as if she were about to burst with fury. "You're not in charge anymore. You said you're not one of us. You said it's *our* problem — not yours. So if it's our problem, *we'll* decide what to do." She moved forward, ready to grab Andrea again.

"Jessie — stop," Leila said, taking Jessie's arm.

Jessie jerked her arm away from Leila. "Shut up!" she screamed.

"*You* shut up!" Ruby yelled.

"Everyone — please!" Leila said, holding both hands up as if she were trying to fend them all off. "We can't decide *anything* if we're just going to scream and threaten each other. We've got to think about this more calmly."

"There's nothing to think about," Andrea said flatly.

"There's a *lot* to think about," Leila said. "Take off your coat, Andrea. Sit down. We're going to discuss this calmly like adults."

Andrea shrugged and sat down without unbuttoning her coat.

"Take off your coat!" Jessie shouted.

Andrea ignored her.

Nina sobbed loudly.

"We've got to think clearly about this," Leila continued. "We can't get carried away. If you will all calm down and take a deep breath, you'll realize that it's all a joke, a ridiculous, stupid joke!"

"It's not a joke," Jessie insisted. "Stop wasting our time by saying it's a joke, Leila."

"Shhhh," Andrea raised a finger to her lips. "I'll tell you what. I'll give everyone time to cool out, time to think quietly about this. You'll see that I'm right. If you're thinking clearly, you'll see that I have no choice. I've got to get to a phone and call the police."

"No! No police!" Rebecca insisted. "Please!"

"Let's go up to our rooms for a short while," Andrea suggested. Her struggle with Jessie and the anger of the other girls had made her seem less certain. Now a pleading tone had entered her voice. "We'll rest for a bit, and think. We'll meet down here at . . . uh . . ." She tried to read her watch, but her arm was shaking too violently. She had to steady it with her other hand.

"How about three o'clock? Okay?"

"And you won't sneak out and go to the police?" Rebecca asked warily.

"Don't worry. She won't," Jessie said menacingly.

"Three o'clock it is," Leila said, and motioned for everyone to get up.

There was a blur of movement in the room. To Abby, it seemed like a slow-motion dream. She stood up, and the room spun slowly around her. Girls moved unsteadily toward the stairway. The fire seemed to leap around the room. Abby thought she saw it burning from the window, then from behind the couch. Fire, fire everywhere.

She blinked and the flames returned to the

fireplace where they belonged. "Now, stay there," she said aloud.

No one seemed to notice.

She pulled Nina to her feet, surprised at how light Nina felt. She put her arm around Nina's tiny waist and began to lead her toward the stairs.

The moose head at the entryway — why was it staring at her? And why was it smiling that toothy, awful grin? She blinked again. The moose head retreated to its sombre, shadowy corner of the wall.

Up the stairs now, one at a time. If only they weren't such a blur. "Nina — please stop crying."

Did Nina hear her? Abby wasn't sure.

And the next thing she knew she was sitting on the bed in a room — somebody's room — her room? — with Nina lying face down, her head buried in the pillow, and Leila, looking concerned, sitting across from her on the bed.

"Leila — " Abby said. "Poor Nina is — "

"Nina, shape up," Leila said softly, reaching down and touching Nina's heaving shoulder. "Nina, come on," Leila said. She grabbed both of Nina's shoulders and turned her around.

"Nina, listen to me. Come on. Look at me," Leila insisted, bending down low so that her face was right above Nina's. "Don't you know this is all a joke? It's a joke, Nina."

"Back off, girl," Jessie suddenly interrupted from the doorway.

Leila ignored her. "Nina — are you listening? They do this every year. I even read about it in the newspaper."

"What?" Nina stopped crying, but her body continued to shake. "What?" She pulled herself up to a sitting position and leaned her head against the headboard. Her hair was wet and tangled from her tears.

"Some fraternity down in Georgia pulls the same thing every year," Leila said brightly. "I read about it a few weeks before school started. So, stop being foolish. It's all a gag. Just a gag."

"A gag?" Nina tried to smile, but her mouth wouldn't cooperate. She fell silent, thinking about what Leila had just said.

Abby looked into Leila's eyes, trying to figure out if Leila was telling the truth about the newspaper story or making it up. But Leila frowned and looked away.

"But — what about Mrs. Driftwood?" Nina asked, tears beginning to flow again.

"Oh come on," Leila said, rolling her eyes. "She gave the worst performance I ever saw! She's in on the gag, Nina. She probably drops dead like that every year for a different group of pledges. You'd think she'd be better at it by now!"

Nina smiled. Her face started to brighten.

"It's not a gag," Jessie said loudly from the doorway.

"What?" Leila challenged, looking at her for the first time.

"You heard me," Jessie sneered. "It's not a gag. The woman was dead. I examined her, remember? You should have seen her face." Jessie closed her eyes and made an ugly face, her version of a corpse.

Nina sank back on the bed and started to cry again.

"Jessie — what's wrong with you?" Leila screamed angrily. "How can you be so cruel?"

Jessie glared back at her, not shrinking at all from Leila's anger. "Death is a part of life," she said quietly, mysteriously.

"I don't see what that has to do with anything," Leila said, looking at Nina. "I was just trying to keep Nina from going completely over the edge. You didn't have to make her crazy again."

"I didn't do anything wrong," Jessie insisted, crossing her arms defiantly. "Telling her it's all a joke isn't going to help her. She has to know the truth."

"But it *is* a joke," Abby suddenly chimed in. "It *has* to be!"

"Get real," Jessie said, and looked out the window.

"She's right," Nina said, startling them all. "Jessie's right. I want to know the truth."

Jessie made a face at Abby and Leila.

"I was telling the truth," Leila insisted.

"I — I'd like to go to my own room," Nina said, climbing off the bed. "I'm starting to feel a little better. At least, I'm starting to think a little clearer."

"I'll take you there," Jessie offered.

"Are you sure you'll be okay?" Abby asked.

"Yeah. Sure. What more could happen?" Nina asked, her voice cracking.

She and Jessie walked together out of the room.

Abby sighed wearily and started to lie down on the bed.

"Don't get comfortable. I want to talk to you," Leila said, her voice quivering.

"What?"

"Not about this stupid sorority prank. I want to talk to you about something real," Leila said. "There's something going on between you and Gordon — *isn't* there!"

Chapter 12

"Leila, you're nuts. Really. I don't know what you're talking about."

Abby turned away, stared at the far wall, and walked quickly past Leila, hoping that Leila couldn't see her face. She sat down at the dressing table with her back to Leila, pulled open the drawer, and fumbled around inside it for her lipstick.

"I think you do know what I'm talking about," Leila said, pronouncing each word slowly and carefully. "I saw the look you gave Gordon when he showed up last night."

Abby struggled not to reveal her true feelings in her voice. "Look? What look? Please, Leila — don't embarrass yourself."

"I saw you, and you *knew* I saw you!" Leila exploded, unable to keep her cool any longer.

"You're being paranoid, Leila."

Abby found a liquid blusher in the drawer and, staring into the dust-smeared mirror, began frantically to apply it. What a joke, she thought. My face is as red as a stop light — and I'm putting on blusher!

"Paranoid? *I'm* paranoid?" Leila was silent for a moment, too angry to speak. Finally, she continued, forcing herself to keep her voice level and calm. "Listen, Abby, let's not kid around. What's the point?"

"I agree."

"I feel bad about what happened last year. But not so bad. I mean, it was Gordon's decision — right? And this kind of thing happens all the time. Kids go together. Kids break up. Kids decide to go with other people. That's what high school is about, I think."

Abby froze her face, not letting any emotion show. She stared at Leila's reflection in the mirror. What is she *talking* about? Abby thought. Kids going together? Breaking up? Doesn't she realize that Gordon and I were in love? And she *ruined* it!

"I — I'm sorry you took it so hard," Leila continued, moving to the window, out of Abby's view in the mirror. "Gordon and I — we didn't think you'd be so . . . upset. But look — that was a year ago."

Leila moved back into Abby's view. She stood right behind Abby's chair, looking at Abby's reflection in the mirror. Abby stared straight ahead, looking back at Leila.

"That was a year ago," Leila repeated. "It's been all over between you and Gordon for a year. Remember that, Abby. I mean it. *You stay away from Gordon!"*

A chill ran up Abby's neck. She spun around, furious. If Leila hadn't taken a step back, Abby would have kicked her.

"Don't you threaten me!" Abby screamed, leaping to her feet, tossing the bottle of blusher at Leila. It sailed over Leila's head and shattered against the wall. "Don't you *ever* threaten me!"

Leila took another step back. She looked surprised. Had she expected Abby just to crumble, or to beg for forgiveness? Maybe she wasn't used to people reacting as furiously as she always did.

"Well ... uh ..." Leila looked at the door, as if planning her escape. "I guess I've said what I have to say."

"I guess you have," Abby said, her cat eyes narrowed in hatred and fury.

"I'm going to see how Nina's doing," Leila said, and walked quickly with long strides out of the room.

When she was gone, Abby slumped back into the chair in front of the dressing table. She had to cry. She needed to cry. "No!" she said aloud. "No. I won't." And she held back the tears, held back the shivers, the chills, held back all of her feelings.

What a horrible day. It was early afternoon, but she felt exhausted, completely drained ... broken. "That's it. I feel broken," she told herself. "Broken. Broken." The word began to repeat itself in her mind until it lost all meaning.

She stared into the mirror. She had to force her eyes to focus. Her face was a blur surrounded by her short, black hair. But then she didn't look too bad. A little lipstick and she'd look just about normal.

Normal?

Another word that had lost all meaning.

Gordon flashed into her mind. Yes, Gordon, she thought. He's probably still here. In this house. He's here.

Suddenly, a familiar voice shattered her vision of him. "What's the matter, Abby? Sorority life getting you down?"

Abby let out a short gasp. "Gabriella! I don't *believe* it! What are *you* doing here?"

"You don't sound glad to see me," Gabriella said, with an exaggerated pout.

"I — I'm just totally shocked."

"You always did shock easily," Gabriella replied. There was no warmth in her tone. She was putting Abby down — as usual.

"How did you get here?" Abby turned to the mirror and picked up her lipstick.

"It wasn't hard to figure out where they were going to take you," Gabriella said.

"But why did you come?" Abby asked impatiently.

"I don't like being left out." Gabriella's reflection grinned at Abby.

Abby was really confused. She gripped the edge of the dressing table and held onto it tightly. "But you can't just come here, Gabriella."

"I'm here," Gabriella said, her grin widening, her dark lips tightly set against her pale white skin.

"But you weren't invited," Abby insisted.

"Invited?" Gabriella laughed, but quickly cut the laugh short. "Don't worry, Abby. I won't embarrass you in front of your classy sorority pals. I didn't come to embarrass you."

Gabriella laughed again, a quiet, dry laugh. "I've come for a very different reason."

"What? What are you talking about? Tell me!" Abby demanded.

Abby spun around, but Gabriella had left the room.

Broken, Abby thought. Broken, broken, broken.

She turned back to the mirror and picked up the lipstick.

Broken, broken, broken.

Looking intently into the mirror, she began applying the lipstick to her lips, lightly at first and then pressing harder and harder. Her hand moved in quick circles, smearing the soft lipstick over her lips, on her chin, under her nose. Round and around. Round and around. She smeared the lipstick in wider and wider circles, covering her lower face, and then her cheeks.

She stared into the mirror, admiring her work. Round and around. Bigger and bigger circles — until her mouth, her chin, her cheeks were all red . . . blood red.

Chapter 13

"The thing to remember is," Jessie said, staring straight ahead at the tall green weeds that blanketed the dune, "that no matter what that idiot Andrea says, we're all in this together."

Nina leaned her head against the wooden back of the rickety, old porch swing and stared up at the sky. Black clouds were rolling in from above the ocean, covering the sun and bringing a wet chill to the afternoon air.

"Looks like it's gonna storm," Nina said quietly. She looked around the large porch that stretched the length of the house. The screens were all torn or missing. There wouldn't be much protection from the rain back here.

"I'm glad you've calmed down," Jessie said, watching a group of sparrows hopping around on the sand under the tall weeds.

"Talking to you helped a lot," Nina said. Jessie wasn't such a bad person, she decided.

She was weird. But she had a certain honesty about her. She was what she was, nothing more or less. And that was refreshing, compared to a lot of other girls Nina knew, with their hang-ups, and disguises, and phony poses.

"What's going to happen?" she asked, looking over to Jessie. "Do you think Andrea will go call the police?"

For some strange reason, Jessie laughed. "No, I don't," she said. She was watching a tall, gray tern pecking at the sparrows' wings with its long beak, trying to chase them away. There was a lot of chirping and rustling of the tall weeds as the unhappy sparrows made their escape. "I wouldn't worry about Andrea." Jessie was being very mysterious.

Nina frowned, watching the tern strut about, enjoying its territorial victory. "Then maybe we'll go home this afternoon," she said.

"Nope. We can't do that," Jessie said. She picked a stone up off the porch and heaved it at the tern. It missed by a mile. The strutting bird pretended not to notice. "The driver took the bus and left until tomorrow night. He had another job on the South Shore this evening."

"You mean we're prisoners here?" The panic slipped back into Nina's voice.

Jessie laughed again. "I guess."

Why did she keep laughing like that? Nina wondered. What was so funny? She watched Jessie throw another pebble at the tern.

"Maybe we should go in," Nina said. "It's getting real dark. It's really going to pour."

"I'm starving," Jessie said. "We forgot about lunch."

Nina looked at her. "How can you think about eating after — after this morning."

"I'm a growing girl," Jessie said, smiling at her warmly. "Let's go down to the kitchen and —"

A loud noise — nearby — caused Jessie to stop. She had started to climb to her feet, but the surprise of the noise sent her sprawling back onto the porch swing. The swing creaked under her weight and hit the back of the porch.

"That was a gunshot!" Jessie cried.

"What?" Nina's mouth dropped open, her lips forming a wide O of fear. "A gun?"

The color returned to Jessie's face. She shook her head as if scolding herself, and laughed again.

"Whew! That scared me. But it's nothing," Jessie said. "Duck hunters, probably. Across the dune. It's duck season, you know."

"Oh. Right." Nina took a deep breath. "Of course. Duck hunters." She shivered. "Let's go in. That wind is so cold."

"Shhh." Jessie raised an arm to hold her back. "Nina — look!" Jessie whispered. She pointed toward the tall weeds at the edge of the dune.

"What is it?" Nina whispered back. But she quickly saw what Jessie was pointing at.

Someone was running through the weeds, bent low, running at full speed. It was a man. At first she thought it was an old man since he was so bent over. Then she realized that a bent-up, old man wouldn't be running that fast.

"Who on earth!?" Jessie whispered, still holding on to Nina.

Nina stared at the running figure. The black clouds shut out all of the sunlight now. It was nearly as dark as night, an eerie darkness, thick grays overlapping dense, somber greens.

But even in the heavy darkness of the approaching storm, Nina recognized the mysterious runner.

"Oh, good lord!" she cried. "It — it's Gordon!"

"What? You *know* him?" Jessie cried. They didn't have to whisper. The wind was strong enough to drown out their voices.

"Well . . . yes. I do!" Nina said, standing up. "It's Gordon. Leila's boyfriend. What is he doing here? And why is he running like that?"

Jessie pulled her broad shoulders up into a shrug. "Weird," she said, and gave Nina a half smile. She looked at her watch, a big, clunky jogger's watch. "Hey — three o'clock. Time to go in and face the music." She laughed as if she had just made a really clever joke.

Nina frowned. What's so funny? she thought.

She opened the screen door and stepped in quickly, glad to be in from the approaching storm. But she knew that the old house held no safety or protection for her, and no escape from the horrors of the morning. The panic returned to the pit of her stomach as she walked quickly up to the living room and to the meeting.

"Who let the fire die down?"

"Well, as you keep reminding us, you were here all day, Ruby," Emily scolded. "You could have tended the fire." She raised a wad of tissues to her nose. She was catching a cold.

"I stayed upstairs," Ruby answered, shrugging. "Besides, no one told me to take charge of the fire."

"Ruby, it's only common sense —" Emily started, but a sneeze interrupted her.

Without saying a word, Rebecca strode quickly over to the fireplace, picked up a handful of kindling, and tossed it onto the dying red embers. She found the long wooden matches in a container on the mantel, and bent down to light the kindling and revive the fire.

"We can't start arguing over silly things like the fire," she said, her little voice sounding hoarse and tired. "We have more important things to decide."

"She's right," Ruby agreed quickly. "I think we all should go with Andrea to the nearest house. We could phone the police and then phone for rides to get us — "

"Leila — " Nina called across the room. Leila looked up. "Did you know that Gordon — "

Leila raised her finger to her lips to shush Nina, and quickly looked away.

A loud rumble of thunder startled them all. It was followed by a powerful rush of wind and the drumming of large raindrops against the window.

"Somebody — close the window!" Emily cried.

"Why don't *you* do it?" Jessie said.

"Why don't *you*? You're closest!" Ruby said nastily.

Abby suddenly felt quite sick. These weren't the same girls who had come out to the house the day before. These weren't the sophisticated sorority sisters she had hoped to be sharing an adventure with. They all looked terrible. And they were acting like a bunch of whiny four-year-olds.

She raised a hand to her chin. It was still a little sore from all the rubbing she had to do to remove the lipstick. Her whole face felt raw and tingly. Of all the silly things!

She looked over at Leila, who was sitting on the floor near the fireplace. Her hair was unbrushed and the back of her sweater was untucked. Even Leila has fallen apart, Abby thought.

Broken.

"Do I have to do *everything*?" Rebecca cried, reaching up her long arms to pull down the rain-spotted window.

"We've got to get out of here," Nina said, holding the sides of her armchair tightly.

"Do *you* want to go out in this?" Emily said, gesturing to the window. The rain was pounding the ground, swirled by the strong winds, accompanied by long roars of thunder. "The next house is at least a mile away."

"No," Nina said quietly, retreating back into her chair.

The lights flickered. Nina and Rebecca shrieked.

"The first thing we have to do," Leila said, getting up and walking over to the fire to warm her hands, "is lighten up."

Rebecca picked up a large birch log with some difficulty and heaved it into the fire, sending up a rush of flames and sparks.

Leila jumped back as sparks flew from the fireplace. She gave Rebecca a dirty look, but Rebecca was busily picking up another log from the basket in the corner and didn't see her.

"The second thing we have to do is to realize that this is *supposed* to be torture time. That's what it's all about."

"Come on, Leila —" Jessie interrupted. But Leila vehemently told her to shush.

"So, we can take our torture like good little girls," Leila continued, turning her back to the fire and staring at Abby for some reason. "Like good little sorority girls, I mean. And then when Andrea tells us it was all a joke, we can tell each other how we knew it all along, and congratulate ourselves for our courage and for making it as Tri Gams, and —"

"But it's not a joke!" Jessie insisted, jumping to her feet, looking as if she might rush forward and attack Leila.

Leila let out an exasperated sigh and rolled her eyes.

"Leila," Nina called quietly, her face buried in shadows, "how can it be a joke?"

"You're kidding yourself, Leila," Jessie said, walking to the window and staring out at the sheets of rain. "You're lying to yourself. Sure, we all *want* it to be a joke. But we don't always get what we want."

"Let me finish what I started to say," Leila said, reaching behind her to tuck in her sweater. "We either play along like we're supposed to. Or we just tell Andrea that the game is over. We don't want to play anymore."

"Hey —" Abby cried loudly. She had been silent the whole time, and everyone jumped at the sound of her voice. "Where *is* Andrea?"

They all looked around the room, as if Andrea might be hiding somewhere watching them. But there was no sign of her.

"She's never late," Leila said, starting to

pace back and forth in front of the fire.

"Sit down, Leila. You're making me nervous," Emily said crossly.

"Your *face* makes *me* nervous!" Jessie cracked.

"Stop it! Stop it!" Abby shouted. She realized immediately from the looks on their faces that she had reacted a little too violently. "We've got to find Andrea," she said, forcing her voice down.

"She probably fell asleep in her room," Leila suggested. "Come on — let's go get her."

Leila headed to the stairway, and they all trooped behind her. A long streak of lightning crackled outside the window, and the lights dimmed and then slowly brightened.

They went down the long hallway, the floorboards creaking beneath their shoes. Andrea's room was the last one on the left. The door was closed .

Leila knocked softly, then harder.

"Andrea? Andrea — wake up."

Silence.

"Open the door!" Nina cried impatiently.

Jessie pushed her way forward, grabbed the big glass doorknob, and turned it. She pushed the door open, and they all began to step inside.

The lamp on the bedtable cast dim yellow light over the large bedroom. "Andrea?" Jessie called.

"Oh no! NO! PLEASE — NO!"

First they saw her white stockinged feet, lying on the floor on the other side of the bed, pointing straight up.

Then they saw the dark pool of blood.

Their screams and cries echoed down the long, empty hallway.

No one moved. Finally, Jessie walked over to the bed and looked down.

"She's — been shot!"

More screams and cries. Abby grabbed onto Nina, trying desperately not to faint to the floor. Nina buried her head in Abby's sweater.

"Is she — dead?" Rebecca managed to whisper, looking away.

"Yes," Jessie said, sounding more angry than upset. "Andrea's dead."

The other girls began to push into the room. "Stay back. Stay back," Jessie warned. "We can't move anything. We can't touch anything. The police won't want anything in the room disturbed."

Then she pushed herself away from the bed and looked up at Leila.

"Still think this is a joke, Leila?"

Chapter 14

"We've got to find a phone. There's *got* to be a phone somewhere in this house."

Rebecca, her face a ghastly yellow in the dim lamplight of the living room, began dashing frantically from table to table, pushing aside vases and lamps, her long, slender hands searching every surface for a phone.

"Rebecca — sit down," Leila called firmly, pointing to a vacant armchair by the fire.

"Ouch!" Rebecca knocked a large glass ash tray off an end table. It bounced heavily off her foot and shattered. Rebecca raised her hands to pull her long red hair, and let out a long, high-pitched shriek.

"Rebecca — " Leila called impatiently. "That isn't doing anyone any good. Try to think of everyone else. We can't start thinking only about ourselves. Now we're *all* really in this together. Every one of us."

Ruby scowled, walked over quickly, and put an arm around Rebecca's waist. Talking to her softly, she led her back to the others, and helped her sit down in the armchair by the fire.

Abby stared down at the shattered ash tray beneath the end table. Broken, she thought. Broken, broken, broken.

And it will never be put back together again.

The rain continued to batter the wide double windows behind them. Outside the windows, the tall weeds of the dune, unable to stand up to the powerful gusts of wind, were crushed flat against the sand as if a steamroller had gone over them.

The lights flickered again, causing several girls to gasp.

Darkness, Abby thought. Soon we will all be cast into darkness.

Jessie disappeared into the kitchen for a moment, then returned with a handful of long, green candles. Just as she began to pass them out, the lights dimmed, darkened, and stayed dark.

"No! I don't believe it! I don't *believe* it!" Rebecca's little voice cried out. They could see her cover her face with her hands in the flickering fire light. Shadows danced and tossed about the room.

"Rebecca — do you want to go upstairs and lie down?" Leila asked.

Matches were struck by shaking hands. Circles of yellow candle light cast an eerie, old-fashioned glow.

"No — please!" Rebecca mistook Leila's

offer as a threat. "Don't make me go up there."

"I'm not *making* you go," Leila said softly. "I thought it might help you to lie down for a bit."

"Not up there," Rebecca said in a shaky voice.

"We have to call the police. We can't just leave Andrea lying up there," Emily said.

"Her parents. Her parents," Nina said between sobs.

"I'm not going out in that storm," Ruby insisted.

"It's safer than staying in here," Rebecca cried. "*Anything* is safer than staying in here! Poor Andrea —"

A howling gust of wind pushed hard against the windows. Their eyes all turned to see if the glass would stand up to it. The window shook, rattled, but didn't break. The wind continued to howl. The ceiling above their heads creaked.

"Abby, why did you get up?" Leila called, raising her candle in front of her to see better.

Abby stared into Leila's candle flame. She hadn't realized she had climbed off the sofa. "One of us is a killer," she said in a flat voice, a dead voice she didn't recognize.

"Abby, please —" Leila started softly.

"No!" Nina suddenly cried out through her sobs and hiccups.

"One of us is a killer," Abby repeated in

her emotionless new voice. "It's *you*, Jessie — isn't it!"

"What?" Jessie cried. "Me?! Why me?!"

"We all saw you threaten Andrea," Abby said in a flat, emotionless tone that made her words even more chilling.

"Yes! That's right!" Rebecca chimed in. "We did! You didn't want her to phone the police because — because you were the one who held the gun!"

"Now, wait — " Jessie started.

"And you brought the gun back. I saw you," Abby added, staring into Jessie's startled face.

"I — I put the gun upstairs," Jessie said, the candle shaking in her hand. "I didn't shoot Andrea or anyone else with it, Abby. How stupid can you be! It's loaded with blanks — remember?"

Abby shook her head. "It *was* loaded with blanks. But bullets can be taken out and new ones put in. . . ."

"No!" Nina cried, jumping to her feet. "Jessie didn't do it! Gordon killed Andrea!" she shouted. And then hiccupped loudly.

"What?" Leila's voice rose several octaves. "What did you say?"

"What?" Abby repeated, a second late. She felt her heart skip at the mention of Gordon's name.

"Gordon killed Andrea." Nina's candle went out. She made no attempt to relight it. She didn't even seem to notice.

"Who is Gordon?" Emily asked.

"Gordon isn't here," Leila said quickly, ignoring Emily. "What's *wrong* with you, Nina? Why would you say a thing like that? Gordon doesn't even *know* Andrea."

"Gordon *is* here, Leila," Nina insisted. "You're lying. Jessie and I saw him. We saw him running over the dune behind the house." Another loud hiccup.

"First we heard a gunshot," Jessie added from the back of the room.

Everyone turned to look at Jessie. With the candle held in front of her face, she looked like a big jack-o-lantern.

"We thought it was duck hunters," Jessie added quickly. "But then we saw this guy — Gordon — running over the dune. He was bent real low, as if he didn't want to be seen."

"Who's Gordon?" Emily repeated.

Darkness, Abby thought. We're being cast into darkness. She blew out her candle, and smiled.

"This is just *silly*!" Leila said, trying hard not to lose control. "Why would Gordon shoot Andrea? I told you, Gordon doesn't *know* Andrea! It *had* to be Jessie! Jessie was ready to kill Andrea right here in the living room. We all saw it!"

"That's right," Abby agreed, a bit too loudly.

"You also told us Gordon wasn't here," Nina said to Leila, hiccupping. "You lied about that, didn't you!"

"Yes, but — "

Leila didn't finish her sentence.

She froze. Everyone froze.

The sounds they heard weren't from the blowing of the wind or the creaking of the old house. The sounds that interrupted them came from the front entranceway.

Someone was banging on the door.

Chapter 15

"Don't answer the door. Please!"

Rebecca dropped her candle. It rolled across the carpet, still lit. Ruby grabbed it up quickly and handed it back to Rebecca.

They heard the loud pounding again, six knocks, hard and insistent.

"We've got to answer the door," Jessie said, walking quickly toward the entrance-way. "It's — it's only the bus driver. I'm sure he's come back to drive us home."

"Yes!" Nina cried, starting to follow Jessie. "Of course it's the bus driver!" The thought seemed to have chased away her hiccups. "Thank God! We can get out of here!"

The small, shimmering circle of light from Jessie's candle led the way to the entrance-way. Almost to the front door, she turned and raised the candle above her head. "Well? Isn't anyone going to come with me? Are you all too chicken?"

The others followed reluctantly, circles of

candlelight trembling before them as they entered the hallway and approached the front door.

Four more knocks, louder this time.

"Coming. We're coming!" Jessie shouted. But she realized whoever was out there probably couldn't hear a thing over the pounding of the rain.

She struggled with the top lock, turned the knob, and pulled open the heavy door.

A burst of wind sent a wave of rainwater into the entranceway. Jessie backed away, too late. She was drenched.

The girls raised their candles to see who was stepping through the doorway.

"Gordon!" Abby cried.

His dark hair was matted against his head. Water dripped down his face. His denim jacket was completely soaked through, as were his jeans. His black boots were mudsplattered and wet. "I got caught in the storm," he said, shivering.

He took a few steps away from the door, leaned forward, and shook himself like a dog, spraying water on them all. Then he stood up, a devilish grin spreading across his dripping wet face.

"Grab him!" Nina cried. "Don't let him get away! He killed Andrea!"

The grin died quickly on Gordon's face. He wiped his wet forehead with an even wetter hand and stared through the dim candlelight to see who was accusing him. A dark puddle of water circled him on the carpet.

"Who?"

"Grab him — quick! He killed Andrea!" Nina screamed.

But no one wanted to touch him. He was too wet.

"Nina — what's the matter?" Gordon asked, sounding confused. He shivered, wrapping his arms around his chest. "Anyone spare a towel?"

"Who *is* he?" Emily asked.

"I'm Gordon," he told her.

"Why did you do it?" Nina screamed, walking up close to him, looking up into his wet face. "Gordon, I've known you for so long! How *could* you?"

Gordon looked down at her. He was at least a foot taller than she. "How could I *what*?" he asked. "Why are you on my case, Nina?"

The lights suddenly revived, flickered back to life. The hallway filled with yellow light.

Nina and Gordon continued to stare at each other.

"What are you saying? That I killed somebody?" Gordon was genuinely confused.

"Don't act so innocent," Jessie suddenly burst in, elbowing Nina out of the way to get up close to Gordon. "We saw you running away. We heard the gunshot. Then we saw you, running in a crouch." She stuck her round face up close to his, challenging him. "I guess you always run like that — right?"

"Well. . . ." Gordon shrugged sheepishly.

He never was much of a talker. Shivering from the cold, struggling to keep the water from runing down into his eyes, confronted by these shrill, screaming girls and their accusations, he was finding it difficult to talk at all.

"Why were you running like that, Gordon?" Nina, hidden behind Jessie, asked quietly.

"I — I guess I didn't want anyone to see me," he said reluctantly.

"I *knew* it!" Nina cried. "Oh, somebody — help! We've got to tie him up or something!"

"Now, cool it, Nina," Gordon said, pushing Jessie out of the way so he could see her. "Have you gone bonkers or something? I'm not confessing to any murder. I just said I didn't want anybody to see me leaving the house."

"You killed Andrea, Gordon!" Nina cried. "We saw you. Jessie and I saw you!"

"You saw him *shoot* her?" Emily asked, bewildered by the change in Nina's story.

"No. We saw him running," Jessie said impatiently. She moved back up to him. "Why didn't you want anyone to see you leave the house?" she asked, sounding tough, like a bad TV detective.

"Well ... I guess. . . ."

"What were you doing here in the first place?" Jessie asked, coming so close Gordon was forced to take a step back.

"He came to see me!"

Everyone turned to see who had spoken

those surprising words.

Abby felt her face turning red. For a second, she wished the lights hadn't come back on. "I admit it," she said, staring into Gordon's eyes. "He snuck into my room last night. He followed me from the campus. He wanted to see me, to be with me. Isn't that right, Gordon?"

Gordon's face twisted in confusion. "Abby — you shouldn't."

"It's okay," Abby said, feeling the heat that reddened her face course through her entire body. "Gordon and I were together last night," she said, unblinking, staring hard into Gordon's eyes.

Look back at me, Gordon. Look back at me with the same feeling I'm sending out to you, Abby thought.

But Gordon looked down at the wet carpet.

"He didn't want anyone to see him leave this afternoon because. . . . because he didn't want to hurt my reputation." She turned away from Gordon and looked at the other girls defiantly, proudly, a triumphant smile on her dark lips.

"No, Abby —" Gordon raised his hand, gesturing for her to stop.

"It's the truth," Abby said, her heart pounding, pounding with gladness, with real happiness. "He was with me the whole time. He didn't kill Andrea. He didn't even —"

"It's not the truth!" Gordon shouted, water spraying off the shoulders of his denim jacket. He looked across the room at Leila and shrugged. "Abby, please. I guess you're just trying to help me. But you might as well tell the truth."

"I *am*!" Abby insisted.

What was the *matter* with him?

Didn't he *know* the truth?

"I came to see Leila," Gordon said, still looking at the carpet. "I was with Leila all night. I didn't wake up till this afternoon. Then I tried to get away without anyone seeing me."

Everyone looked at Leila, who nodded agreement.

"No, no, no," Abby insisted, grabbing Gordon's shoulder and pushing him back. "Don't you know it's all broken? Everything's broken!"

Surprised by her push, Gordon stumbled backwards. He regained his balance by putting a hand up onto the wall. "What?" he asked. "What did you say?"

"I — I don't remember," Abby said. She really didn't remember. Suddenly she felt very upset. Everything had been so nice, so right. Everything had been so clear to her.

So why couldn't she remember what she had just said?

Leila stared hard at Abby, reading the confusion on her face. Poor, confused Abby,

Leila thought. Poor Abby. She really believes what she's saying. . . .

Suddenly, Leila found herself trembling all over. Tears welled in her eyes. Poor Abby. Poor, confused Abby.

What's happening to me? Leila thought. Why do I feel so strange?

Staring at Abby, she answered her own questions. In that instant, Leila realized that she still cared about her old friend a great deal. Abby was not a threat to her, she realized. Abby was in trouble.

Abby and I were such good friends, she thought. We were like sisters.

Surprised at her own emotions, at the strong feelings she still had for Abby — feelings she had held back for more than a year — Leila felt her anger lift, felt her guilt fade away.

Poor Abby, she repeated to herself. Poor, confused Abby.

"Someone isn't telling the truth here," Jessie said, interrupting Leila's thoughts. Jessie moved forward to take charge, giving Abby a strange look. She grabbed Gordon's arm and forced it behind him. "Come on — up you go. We're locking you in a bedroom upstairs till we can get help."

Gordon made no effort to resist. "Fine," he said quietly.

"This is *stupid*!" Leila cried, moving forward to pull Jessie away.

But Gordon raised a hand to stop her. "It's

okay," he said. "Look — I just came in to get dry. If you want to put me in some room — fine. I'm not gonna fight you."

"But there's no reason — " Leila started.

"A nice, dry room sounds fine to me," Gordon said. "I didn't shoot anybody. I've never held a gun in my life. I didn't do anything. So go ahead — take me upstairs. Lock me up. Just give me a towel — okay? And maybe a dry bathrobe or something?"

"Gordon!" Leila seemed positively furious that he was giving in to them.

Jessie, still bending Gordon's arm behind his back, pushed him toward the steps. "I'm locking him in the empty bedroom," she called down.

No one knew what to say.

They all stood in the entranceway for a few moments. Then they slowly began to drift back to the living room. Rebecca moved to tend to the fire, which had died to dull, red embers.

Leila walked up quickly to Abby, tenderly put a hand on her shoulder, and pulled her close, whispering in her ear. "Abby — you and I should do some talking — about Gordon."

Abby jerked herself out of Leila's grip. Her green cat eyes flared up as if on fire, and her dark lips formed a tight sneer. "I want to talk to you too, Leila. Come up to my room — *now*!"

Chapter 16

"What's *wrong* with me? I can't stop crying."

Nina pulled a bunch of tissues from the box Jessie held out to her.

"You're lucky," Jessie said, tossing the box onto the bed beside Nina. "You can let out your emotions."

"What good is *that*?" Nina asked, the tears beginning to fall down her swollen, red cheeks again. "Everyone just thinks I'm a baby."

Jessie started to contradict her, but Nina shook her head and gestured for her not to say anything.

"The whole reason . . . the whole reason I wanted to join, to be a Tri Gam," Nina said from behind her wad of tissues, "was to be sophisticated . . . you know — mature. And all I've done is cry like an infant!" She tossed the wet tissues angrily down on the bed. "I can't help it. I'm *so* upset!"

Jessie walked over to the crushed velvet armchair beside the closet and picked up her big bookbag. She searched through it, pawing intently, until she found what she was looking for. She grinned as she pulled out a Three Musketeers bar.

"Big enough to share with a friend," Jessie said, tearing off the wrapper and tossing it on the floor. "Want half?"

Nina moaned. "I couldn't. Thanks. I just keep thinking about Andrea, lying there two doors down. . . . That blood all over the floor.... Uh-oh. Here I go again." She reached for another handful of tissues as the loud, uncontrollable sobs resumed.

Jessie took a big bite of the candy bar, then another. "What can I say to calm you down?" she said, chocolate all over her teeth. "You know *I* didn't do it, don't you? I was with *you* the entire time."

"Yes, I know," Nina said through her tears.

"Well . . . you've got to remember you're not the only one who's in this mess. You're not responsible. We're all to blame for whatever's happened."

Nina looked up at her, but didn't reply.

"So why do you want all the guilt on *your* shoulders?" Jessie continued, taking another big bite of the candy bar. "Why do you want to do all the crying for us?"

"What are you accusing me of?" Nina cried, sitting up quickly. "I'm not crying because I want to take everyone's guilt! Who asked *you* to be my shrink, anyway?"

"Now, wait — " Jessie started.

"I'm crying because I'm *upset!*" Nina

shouted. "Upset, upset! It's normal to cry when you're upset. Some terrible things have happened here. People are dead! It's normal to cry when people — "

Nina stopped suddenly and stared at Jessie. Her mouth dropped open. She looked surprised by her own thoughts.

"Wait a minute," Nina said slowly, her eyes narrowing. "How come *you're* so calm, Jessie?"

"I told you," Jessie said, setting down the remaining half of the candy bar on the dresser. "Some people can let out their emotions. Some can't."

"You've been so calm through this whole thing," Nina continued, ignoring Jessie's feeble reply. "You haven't cried. You haven't seemed frightened or upset. Not for more than a minute or two, anyway."

Nina stared at Jessie. "Don't you *have* any feelings? Are you so twisted that you don't care about people at all?"

"Nina — that's not fair!" Jessie said, crossing her arms in front of her chest. "Now, stop."

But Nina wasn't finished. She had another thought. "Maybe that isn't it at all," she said thoughtfully. "Maybe there's another reason why you're so calm, Jessie. You know what? I think you know more about what's been going on this weekend than you're letting on."

Jessie turned away and looked out the window. A mysterious smile spread over her face. "You're out of your mind. . . ." she said quietly.

Leila lifted the large green mug to her lips, took a long sip of the hot tea, and burned her mouth. She slammed the mug down on the kitchen table, startling a few of the other girls.

I have to do something about Abby, she thought.

But what?

After Gordon had been safely locked upstairs, someone realized they hadn't eaten since breakfast. Rebecca hurried to the kitchen to make a pot of tea. Emily, still mostly in a daze, began opening cabinet doors, looking for some ingredients to make pancakes. The others had scattered all over the house.

Several minutes later, the tea had been made and poured. But Emily was still staring into cabinets, unsuccessful in her quest, seemingly unable to come up with an alternate plan.

What am I going to do? Leila thought. A dozen scenes rushed through her mind, ugly pictures, upsetting pictures of what had taken place in the last few hours. She saw Mrs. Driftwood in her shop. She saw the gun in Jessie's hand. She saw the old lady's face begin to twitch. Saw her clutch her chest and fall. She saw Andrea, or rather, Andrea's stocking feet, lying in a dark pool of blood, the blood soaking onto her white socks.

Then she saw Gordon climbing into her bedroom window. She saw Abby rush forward to greet him. Saw the look on Abby's face. The way she raised her arms to him.

Abby was still in love with him. Still crazy about him.

Still . . . crazy.

But how crazy? Crazy enough to think that Gordon might come back to her?

Leila decided she had to confront Abby. She had to make sure that Abby knew the truth — for Abby's sake.

Two people were dead. For real? Were they really dead? Leila had been so certain that it had all been a sorority prank, so certain that it was all a put-on. But now . . . she just didn't know what to think.

It was easier to think about Abby. And Gordon.

Leila took another long sip of tea, ignoring how hot it was. She felt empty. And cold. She wanted to run upstairs to Gordon. He would know how to make her feel warm, warm and comfortable.

But Gordon was locked up in the empty bedroom.

Those idiots, idiots. Leila's thoughts turned angrier. How can they be so stupid? I know Gordon. He looks tough, sure. He looks kinda punky. But he isn't really.

He's a marshmallow, she thought.

Why did he give in to them so easily? Why

did he let himself be dragged up to that bedroom? Why didn't he fight them just a little?

Because he's a marshmallow.

He didn't kill Andrea. He couldn't kill anyone.

Then who did?

Was it Jessie?

It could have been. . . .

Jessie had been so gung-ho about this whole adventure. Jessie *wanted* to carry the gun. Jessie *wanted* to commit the crime. Jessie was the least upset of any of them. In fact, Jessie wasn't upset at all.

It was Jessie.

She didn't want Andrea to call the police.

But did she want to stop her badly enough to kill her?

No. That was ridiculous.

Jessie didn't kill Andrea.

But then, who did? One of the other girls?

I've got to stop these crazy thoughts, Leila told herself. She took one last gulp of tea, pushed her chair away from the table, and walked out of the kitchen.

She realized she was shivering. The tea hadn't warmed her at all. Thunder rattled outside the front door. The rain, which had slowed for a while, picked up once again.

She hesitated at the bottom of the stairs, listening to the rain, gathering her strength. Then slowly she began to climb.

It was time to go up and have a chat with Abby.

Chapter 17

Leila paused for a moment outside Gordon's room. She put her ear up close to the door and listened.

Silence.

Knowing Gordon, he had probably climbed under the covers to get warm, and had immediately fallen asleep!

She suddenly remembered the first time Gordon had come to her house. He was grudgingly taking her to some sort of school dance, and she had been so eager for her parents to meet him.

He allowed himself to be ushered into the den, and the usual small talk had followed. Leila was upstairs, having trouble getting her hair right. They heard a noise in the basement. Leila's parents excused themselves for a moment to go see what the trouble was — and when they returned a few minutes later, there was Gordon, sound asleep on the den couch!

Her parents had referred to him as Rip Van Winkle ever since, and joked about how lazy and sleepy he always was. When Gordon didn't go to college in September, and didn't have a job either, their jokes about him became serious. Leila finally had had enough — and, during a screaming fight, had demanded that they stop bugging her about him. Her parents, who were just as frightened of Leila's temper as her friends were, immediately agreed to her demand. Gordon was never mentioned in the house again.

Sighing, Leila stood at the bedroom door, listening to the silence for a few more seconds.

She wished she were in there with him.

Shaking her head sadly, she walked next-door to the room she shared with Abby.

Calm, girl. Be calm, she told herself. Just make everything clear to her. Say what you have to say, and split. Don't let it get emotional. Don't upset her — or yourself. You can handle it, Leila. You've *got* to.

I tried being nice to her, Leila thought. I really tried. I tried to pretend that we could be friends again. I didn't want to make her uncomfortable. So I pretended.

Now . . . no more pretending.

Leila took a deep breath and pushed open the heavy door to the bedroom. All of the lights had been turned on. Abby was seated at the dressing table. Her back was turned to Leila: She seemed to be staring into the ornate, oval mirror in front of her, not moving, just staring at her reflection. Her hair had been carefully brushed. Leila could see in the mirror that she had put on fresh lipstick and eye makeup.

"Abby — it's me," Leila said softly.

Abby didn't move.

"Abby?" Leila called, taking a few steps into the room.

For a second, she imagined that Abby was dead, murdered at her dressing table by the same person who had murdered Andrea.

But Abby slowly turned around.

Abby's green eyes opened wide, not in surprise, but in pleasure. She grinned at Leila, a weird, lopsided grin.

"Abby — are you okay?"

At least ten seconds passed before Abby answered. "I'm not Abby," she said finally, in a hoarse voice. "I'm Gabriella."

Chapter 18

Leila gripped the back of an armchair. "What?"

"You heard me," Abby snapped in the new voice. Her crooked smile spread across her face as if she were celebrating some sort of triumph.

"Now, listen, Abby —" Leila stayed behind the armchair, using it as a shield, afraid to come any closer.

"I *told* you. I'm not Abby. Abby is gone. I'm her sister. Gabriella."

"Abby doesn't have a sister," Leila said softly. She immediately regretted saying it.

"I AM HER SISTER!" Abby, in a rage, jumped up from the small chair. She tossed her head back, her smooth, black hair flowing with it. "I am her loyal sister," she said, spending a long time on the word *loyal*.

"Gabriella?" Leila, trying not to be obvious, looked toward the door.

Should she make a run for it?

How could this all be happening in a house with no telephone? A dead girl in one room, Gordon locked up in another — and a crazy girl in this room!

It's a nightmare, Leila thought. A nightmare with no escape.

Running out of the room wouldn't help matters, she decided. Maybe she could calm Gabriella. Soothe her. Maybe she could get Abby back.

"Listen, Abby — "

"STOP CALLING ME THAT!"

"I'm sorry. I meant Gabriella."

Leila was thinking hard. How should she talk to her? What should she say?

She had seen cases of split personality on TV, in movies — but she never imagined she would ever really be in a room with someone who had suddenly assumed a new identity, a whole new personality, a new voice.

"I am Abby's loyal sister," Gabriella repeated, speaking slowly, in a purring, catlike voice. "And I don't like what you did to my sister."

"I am your sister's friend," Leila said, also talking slowly.

"No, you're not." Gabriella's words came out bitter. Her chin trembled. She looked for a second as if she might weaken. But her eyes pierced into Leila's, cold and hard.

"I think you should pay for what you did to my sister," Gabriella said flatly, without any emotion at all.

"But I didn't *do* anything," Leila protested weakly.

"It wasn't right to steal my sister's boyfriend."

Leila felt as if she were dropping down a dark pit, a dark, bottomless pit. She would never stop falling. This conversation would never end. Down, down, down — until they both disappeared into the darkness.

"I don't know what to say," Leila said, feeling her knees start to collapse. She gripped the chair back tighter and leaned against the back of the chair.

"Say *something*," Gabriella urged, grinning, a grin of pure menace.

"I didn't steal your sister's boyfriend. I didn't steal Gordon. It — it just happened."

Gabriella stared back at her, unmoved.

Was she waiting for Leila to say more?

What more could Leila say?

"*Things like that happen all the time, you know!*" Leila heard herself blurt out. "And people don't go crazy from it!"

No. No. Why had she said that?!

Leila struggled to get back in control.

It would do no good to have *two* crazy girls in the room.

"What did you say?" Gabriella asked, more of a threat than a question.

"Nothing. I didn't mean — " Leila looked toward the door again.

This wasn't going at all well. She didn't seem to be soothing Gabriella at all. In fact, she was getting her more worked up.

Perhaps the best idea now was to run. Run out the door. Run away. Run far away.

How far? How far can I run? Leila asked herself.

Away from this house? Away from these girls? From this mess? From — everything?

Yes. Run. Goodbye, Gabriella. Goodbye, poor crazy Abby.

She turned back to look at Gabriella one more time before making her escape — and saw Gabriella approaching with something in her hand.

A gun.

The pistol. Nina's pistol from the robbery.

Gabriella smiled, seeing the fear spread across Leila's face. "My sister was very upset by what you did," she said. "Very upset."

"Gabriella, wait — "

"In fact, my sister had to go away for a while — because of you."

"No. Really. She — "

"That's when I promised Abby. That's when I promised Abby I'd take care of her." Gabriella took a few steps toward Leila. "And that's when I promised Abby I'd take care of *you*!"

Leila glanced quickly to the door. If she leaped, if she dived, she could get there in two seconds. She could be out of the room and —

Wait a minute, Leila thought. She remembered something suddenly — something important. Something lucky.

"The pistol — it isn't loaded, remember? It's got blanks," Leila said, backing away from the armchair, preparing to make her getaway.

"No, no, no," Gabriella said, and laughed. "I brought the real thing, Leila. Real bullets. Here. I'll show you."

Gabriella raised the pistol and aimed it at Leila's head.

Her hand was as steady and unwavering as her stare.

Without taking her eyes off her target, she pulled back the hammer and lowered her finger to the trigger.

"Here, Leila. I'll show you."

"NO!" Leila screamed. "NO! GABRIELLA — PUT DOWN THE GUN! *PLEASE!*"

Chapter 19

Nina walked over to the living room window and pressed her forehead to the cool glass. She stared at the orange flames from the fireplace reflected in the glass. Outside, the rain had slowed to a misty drizzle. The sky was black and starless, the kind of black you only see far from any town, the kind of black that could roll over you, surround you, swallow you up.

For some reason, she thought of her room back home with its yellow, flowered wallpaper and lacy white curtains. Her parents hadn't touched it since Nina had moved into the dorm.

Nina smiled as she watched the reflection of the flickering flames. A gust of wind shook the low hedge outside the window. Maybe she had been in too big of a hurry to move into the dorm. Maybe she should have lived at home for one more year. Going to college was such a major change. Maybe she didn't need the added pressure of living on her own. Or — even worse — living with Leila!

Leila. Nina turned from the window and searched the quiet living room for her roommate. Emily was sitting silently on the sofa, staring into the fireplace. Ruby and Rebecca were feeding kindling to the fire. Jessie was in the dining room, slurping up a bowl of corn flakes. Leila wasn't in her usual place — the big, overstuffed armchair across from the sofa.

She must still be upstairs, Nina thought.

Maybe she sneaked in to spend some time with Gordon.

Or maybe she was with Abby. Abby wasn't in the room, either.

What was Abby trying to prove with that speech about Gordon coming to see her? Nina asked herself. Was she just trying to provoke Leila? If so, I'm sure she succeeded.

What was the point of it? Did she say all that to try to protect Gordon? It was a pretty lame attempt. Abby didn't *really* believe that Gordon had come to see her — did she?

Nina turned back to the window. She forced herself to stop thinking about Leila and Abby. She didn't want to start sobbing again. It had taken her so long to get in control.

She thought of her bedroom at home again. The flowery wallpaper will have to go, she told herself.

No. She shook her head. No.

I'm not moving back home. I'm just upset. I'm out for good. I'm on my own. No way I'm going back to being a kid. I'm going to be a

Tri Gam and live in the Tri Gam house, the best house on campus.

It made her feel good to stand up to herself, to defeat her weaker impulses. It made her realize that she was stronger than she thought, stronger than she gave herself credit for.

It would be nice just to talk to her parents, though.

Looking down, she saw the cord.

She stared at it for a long while before it clicked into her brain what she was seeing.

A telephone cord.

If there's a cord, maybe there's a phone.

The cord ran along the floor molding. Nina quickly dropped to her hands and knees and began to follow it, squeezing behind curtains and chairs.

"Nina — what are you doing?" Rebecca called from beside the fireplace.

"A phone cord!" Nina told her, pushing her way through a thick spiderweb filled with dead flies. "I found a phone cord!"

"It's probably just an old cord. Andrea told us there were no phones," Jessie called from the dining room.

"It doesn't *look* old," Nina called up to them. "Help me look."

"You're wasting your time," Jessie called, with a mouthful of cereal.

But Emily, Ruby, and Rebecca joined Nina down on the floor. They followed the phone cord the length of the living room. In the corner beside a large, mahogany breakfront, the cord ended in a phone jack.

"Look — it's a modern jack, the kind you just plug in," Rebecca said.

"That means there was a phone here fairly recently," Nina said. "Come on — let's follow the cord in the other direction."

"Do you think there's been a phone here all along?" Emily asked, showing a spark of life for the first time since they had returned from town.

"Why would Andrea lie to us?" Jessie asked, walking quickly into the room. "She said there was no phone."

"Maybe she wanted to scare us," Ruby said. And then, remembering the scene in Andrea's room upstairs, she added quietly, "Poor Andrea."

"We'll call the police first," Nina said, scurrying along the baseboard, following the gray cord out of the living room and into the dining room. "Then we'll call our parents."

Suddenly, they all froze in place. "Did you hear a crash?" Emily asked.

They listened for a few seconds.

"I thought I heard a crash upstairs," Emily said.

They listened again. Silence. They decided to continue tracking down the telephone.

They traced the cord behind an oak cabinet, turned the corner, and followed it into the kitchen, where it disappeared behind a long formica counter.

"Now what?" Rebecca asked.

"See if it comes out the other side," Nina said. They scurried around the counter. "Yes! Look — it — "

Nina stopped because she saw the end of the phone cord. It was resting on the other end of the kitchen counter. There was no phone attached to it.

She felt more anger than disappointment. "There *was* a phone here!" she cried. "Somebody must've hid it!"

"Maybe it's in a closet or a cabinet or something," Emily suggested.

"Let's search everywhere," Nina said. "We've *got* to find it. We've just *got* to!"

She pulled open the cabinet doors above the counter top and stood on tiptoes to see what was inside. Cups and saucers. Dozens of them. She slammed the doors shut.

"Spread out, everyone," Rebecca said. "It could be anywhere."

As Nina moved to the next cabinet, the other girls started to leave the kitchen.

But they stopped at the doorway when they heard the screams.

"I — I think they're coming from the *basement*!" Rebecca stammered, her little mouse voice barely a whisper.

A few minutes earlier, Gabriella had flicked on the light over the steps to the basement. She gave Leila a hard shove in the back with the nuzzle of the pistol. "Down," she said in her throaty, hatred-filled voice. "Quickly."

Leila peered down into the basement. What was scampering across the gray floor? Rats?

As she started reluctantly down the narrow, wooden steps, she inhaled the musty basement air, cold and wet. She stumbled and started to fall, but caught herself at the last moment, gripping the damp, wooden bannister that ran along the stairway.

She felt the pistol press into her back again. "Gabriella — please."

"Get down those stairs," Gabriella whispered, pronouncing each word slowly and carefully.

"I'm going as fast as I can!"

"Shut up — or I'll shoot you right here!" Gabriella threatened.

The fury in her whisper told Leila that it wasn't an empty threat. Her heart pounding, Leila stepped into the basement. Again she heard the scratching of little feet against the concrete floor. She shuddered and hugged herself without realizing it.

Wake up, Leila. *Please* — wake up from this nightmare!

A dust-encrusted bulb hung down from the ceiling. Gabriella pulled the string and it came on, throwing dim yellow light over the large, cluttered area.

Stacks of brown, rotting newspapers lined the far wall. Old furniture was strewn everywhere, cracked tables, a broken vase, an armchair with one leg broken off and its cushion missing. The stench of mildew was over-powering. From somewhere across the room, the steady drip-drip-drip of rainwater seeping into the basement accompanied the sound of scampering rats.

"I — I feel sick," Leila said.

Gabriella laughed.

"What — what are you going to do? Why did we have to come down here?"

Maybe if I keep talking to her, she'll snap out of it, come to her senses, Leila thought. If I just keep talking long enough, she'll go back to being Abby, she'll let me get out of this horrible basement, she won't shoot me.

"Why don't you answer my questions?" Leila asked, unable to keep the desperation from her voice. "Why did you bring me down here?"

"Why do you think?" Gabriella answered, stepping over a wet clump of rags. "I don't want them to find you."

"Find me?" Leila gasped.

"They won't think of looking down here," Gabriella said, suddenly sounding pleased with herself. She laughed again. "They'll probably think you ran away — you know, off into the woods or across the dunes or something. They'll think you escaped."

"But, Gabriella. You — "

Gabriella gestured with the pistol. "Get back against the newspapers."

"But they're wet — " Leila protested.

"Couldn't we sit down upstairs and talk this over? Really!"

Ignoring her question, Gabriella gestured again with the pistol. Her green cat eyes caught the yellow light. Her mouth twisted into a dark red sneer. "They'll think you escaped," she repeated. "But you won't escape, Leila. You won't escape."

"You — you're going to kill me?"

No reply.

"But why, Gabriella? Why?"

Silence. Then . . . "One more murder won't matter, will it?"

"You mean — Andrea? Did *you* kill Andrea?"

No reply.

Gabriella raised the pistol.

"But they'll hear you, Gabriella," Leila said, raising her hands over her face. "They'll hear the shot. They'll come down here. They'll catch you."

"I closed the door behind us," Gabriella said, smiling again. "I'm a smart girl," she said, practically purring. "They won't hear. No one will hear."

Leila kept her hands in front of her face. "Don't do it. Please. Don't shoot."

"I have to," Gabriella said. "I promised my sister. I can't break a promise — can I?"

"If only we could — "

Leila heard the click of the pistol hammer being pulled back.

"Goodbye, Leila," Gabriella said.

149

Chapter 20

"Stop, Abby! Put down the gun!"

Leila lowered her hands from her face. "Gordon! How did you —"

Gabriella didn't move. She stared straight ahead, holding the gun steady, aimed at Leila's chest. "Go back upstairs, Gordon," she said through clenched teeth, not moving her eyes from Leila.

"Gordon — do as she says. The bullets are real!" Leila screamed. Her mouth was dry. Her knees felt weak and rubbery. She began to feel dizzy and faint.

"Please, Abby. Hand me the gun," Gordon said softly, taking a step forward.

"I'M NOT ABBY!" Gabriella shouted. "Are you as blind as you are stupid!"

Gordon shook his head sadly and looked at Leila. "This is what happened to her before," he told her. "This is her other personality."

"What are you talking about?" Gabriella asked, looking away from Leila to glare angrily at Gordon. She lowered the gun for a second, but quickly raised it.

"The gun, Abby." Gordon stretched out his hand.

"Go away, Gordon. This has nothing to do with you," Gabriella said, staring back at Leila.

"I'm not going, Abby — until you give me the gun," Gordon said. He was trying to keep his voice low and calm, but he sounded scared.

Gabriella frowned. "I promised my sister, Gordon. I can't break my promise. I'm not like you."

"Listen, Abby — "

"Gabriella. Gabriella. Gabriella."

"Listen, Gabriella — "

"Shut up, Gordon. You broke your promise — didn't you?"

"I don't know what you mean. Please — " Gordon took another step closer and stopped.

"You broke your promise to my sister. You broke all your promises to my sister." Gabriella's frown was suddenly replaced by a crooked smile. Holding the gun on Leila, she looked at Gordon. "Maybe I'll kill you, too," she said, grinning.

Gordon took another step toward her.

"Gordon — don't!" Leila called. Her head was spinning. She didn't know how much longer she could stand with her back up against the wet newspapers, inhaling the stench. "Go back!"

"No — stay," Gabriella said, moving the pistol suddenly, aiming it at Gordon's chest. "Stay. Stay. Stay. The more the merrier. Ha ha! I have lots of bullets. Lots and lots and lots of bullets."

Gordon, his hand outstretched, his eyes on the pistol that was now aimed at him, took one more step toward Gabriella. "Hand me the gun. Please — Gabriella."

"You broke your promise, Gordon. Broken, broken, broken. Everything is broken now. Goodbye. Goodbye, Leila. Goodbye, Gordon." Gabriella spoke in a low monotone, repeating the word "goodbye" over and over.

Suddenly her expression changed. "Hey — how'd you find us down here?" she asked him.

Gordon took another step, his hand still outstretched and open. "I was in the bedroom next to yours. I heard you arguing. I heard the whole thing. I heard you tell Leila you were taking her to the basement. So I broke down the door and — "

"And you came running down to rescue your poor, precious Leila?" Gabriella interrupted.

Leila desperately shook her head no, hoping Gordon would see her.

"Uh . . . no . . ." Gordon said, thinking hard. "I came down to . . . uh . . . find Abby. I thought Abby would be here."

Gabriella looked confused. "Abby? Why would Abby be here? Why did you want to see Abby?"

"To . . . uh . . . talk to her.'·

"Liar!" Gabriella shouted. "You're lying. Your promise was broken. Broken, broken, broken. And now . . ." she aimed the gun at Gordon's chest ". . . you will be broken, too."

"No!" Leila screamed. She tried to run toward Gabriella, but her knees wouldn't cooperate, and she stumbled and fell hard onto the cold, concrete floor.

Gabriella swung around and pointed the pistol down at Leila. Leila struggled to get back to her feet.

Taking advantage of the distraction, Gordon moved quickly. He leaped forward, diving toward Gabriella. With a loud groan, he made a desperate grab for the pistol — and it went off in her hand.

Chapter 21

"Who's screaming?"

"It sounds like — Leila!"

"In the basement?"

Nina didn't want to stop the hunt for the missing telephone. The phone cord was her first glimmer of hope that there might be a way to summon help, a way to bring an end to this horrible weekend.

But she knew she wasn't imagining the screams. They were real. The other girls heard them, too. Emily pressed her hands over her ears, trying to shut out the sounds.

"It *is* Leila!" Nina decided.

What was she screaming?

It sounded like, "No, Gabriella, no!" But *who* was Gabriella?

Rebecca, her eyes wild with fear, frantically pulled out a drawer from the counter beside the sink. She pulled too hard, and the drawer fell to the floor with a crash that made everyone jump.

Rebecca quickly recovered and picked a

big, black-handled bread knife from the drawer. "Let's go," she whispered.

They followed her to the door to the basement. "Look — the light is on down there," Nina said.

For some reason, Emily still had her hands pressed against her ears.

"I — I'm not going down there," Ruby said, dark circles under her dark, frightened eyes. "Andrea's dead. I . . . we . . . don't want to be next."

They heard angry voices downstairs and sounds of a scuffle.

"Who's down there?" Rebecca called, brandishing the breadknife in front of her.

No reply.

"Who's down there?" Rebecca repeated, trying to shout. But her voice still came out a whisper.

"We can't just stand here on the steps," Jessie broke in from the top of the stairs. Nina turned quickly to look at her. Jessie had an odd expression on her face. She seemed more confused than frightened.

"You can't expect anyone to hear you with your tiny voice," Jessie told Rebecca. She pushed her way past Emily and Ruby. Then she cupped her hands around her mouth and shouted, "WHO'S DOWN THERE?"

That's when they heard the gunshot.

"No!" Emily screamed. "No! No! No!"

Ruby turned and began running up the stairs. Jessie squeezed past Nina and began pushing Rebecca down the stairs ahead of her, holding her by the shoulders. "Come on. Come on, Rebecca. You've got the knife."

Nina's throat tightened until she could barely breathe. But somehow she forced her legs to carry her down into the dark, wet basement. She and Emily followed behind as Jessie continued to push Rebecca toward the sound of scuffling.

The first thing the girls saw was the pistol.

It was lying in the middle of the floor in front of a torn armchair. A few yards behind it, Gordon and Abby were wrestling on the ground, cursing, pulling at each other's hair, rolling on the wet floor, screaming, struggling to reach the gun.

"Let go of me, you creep! Let go of me!" Abby was shrieking. She pounded her fists on Gordon's chest. He grabbed her hands and tried to pull them behind her. But she rolled out of his grasp, dived for the pistol, and missed.

With a leaping tackle, Gordon dragged Abby back down to the floor. Bringing his knee up into her back, he grabbed her arms roughly and pulled them behind her.

"Ouch! OUCH! STOP!!" Abby screamed. She tried to reach her head back to bite at him, but he was holding her at too great a distance.

"Gordon! Gordon! Gordon!"

Someone in the shadow of the wall was screaming.

Staring into the darkness, Nina saw Leila, leaning against the stack of old newspapers, her hands tearing at her tangled hair.

"Gordon! Gordon! Gordon!"

Abby struggled to duck out of Gordon's grasp. He jerked her hard, holding her arms tightly, until she cried out in pain.

"Gordon — what are you *doing*?" Nina screamed.

Was it true? Had Gordon *really* been the one who killed Andrea? And was he trying to kill Abby now?

Nina didn't know what to think.

She saw Rebecca, the big knife wavering in her trembling hand. Jessie stood at her side, still looking confused. Emily hid behind one of the old armchairs. Ruby was at the foot of the basement steps, ready to run back up to safety.

Suddenly, Nina knew what she had to do. Walking quickly, she got to the pistol, picked it up, and aimed it at Abby and Gordon.

"Let her go, Gordon," she said, trying to sound firm.

Startled, Gordon looked up at her. "Nina — you don't understand —"

"Let go of Abby," Nina shouted, holding the pistol in both hands to keep it steady.

"I'M NOT ABBY!" Abby shrieked. "I'M NOT ABBY!" Like a frightened animal caught in a trap, she pulled and pulled, struggling to free herself from Gordon's grasp.

"Gordon — let her go," Nina repeated, but her voice revealed her uncertainty.

"Put down the gun, Nina," Gordon groaned, his face bright red from his efforts to subdue Abby. "Please — "

"But why are you doing that to Abby?" Nina insisted, taking a step back.

"I'M NOT ABBY! I'M GABRIELLA! I'M GABRIELLA!"

Nina lowered the gun. She suddenly realized what was happening. She shook her head sadly. "Poor Abby," she said. "Poor Abby." She looked down into the angry, distorted face of her old friend.

"I'm ... not ... Abby."

"Poor Abby," Nina repeated.

Nina's soft words seemed to affect Abby. She closed her eyes. Her shoulders slumped. She bowed her head. She stopped struggling.

She gave up.

"Gordon! Gordon — are you okay?" Leila came running out of the shadows. She pulled Gordon to his feet and threw her arms around him. Her fear burst out of her in a torrent of words. "Are you okay, honey? Did she hurt you? When that gun went off, I just froze. I was so afraid. But you're okay, honey? You're okay?"

"Yeah. I guess," Gordon managed to say. He lowered his head onto Leila's shoulder, trying to catch his breath, waiting for his heart to stop pounding against his chest.

"I'll kill you, Leila," Abby said quietly,

without looking up. She was still on her knees, her head down. "I'll kill you." A smile spread across her face.

"Abby —" Nina started. "Is there anything I can do? Anything I can do to help?"

But Abby was in her own world. She didn't seem to hear Nina.

"I'm Gabriella," she said in her throaty voice. "Gabriella. Not Abby. I killed Andrea. And I killed Mrs. Driftwood."

There was a long silence. No one moved.

Abby's smile grew wider. She raised her head and grinned up at Leila. "I can kill you too, Leila."

Leila gasped and held Gordon tighter.

"I don't *believe* this!" Jessie exclaimed, shaking her head. "I just don't believe it. Really."

"We've got to get help right away," Nina said, ignoring Jessie. "The storm has stopped. I'll walk to the nearest house."

"I'll go with you," Rebecca and Emily said at the same time.

"That won't be necessary," a voice called from the stairway.

Everyone turned around to see who it was. It was Andrea.

Chapter 22

Emily and Ruby both shrieked.

Rebecca slumped down onto the moldy sofa.

"Andrea!"

"You're alive!"

"But how??"

Andrea walked up to them, smiling. "I guess the game is over. You girls did great. Well . . . maybe not great. But at least you survived."

"But Andrea — " Nina started.

Andrea turned back to the stairway. "You can come down now!" she called.

They all heard light footsteps on the stairs.

A few seconds later, a grinning Mrs. Driftwood appeared.

"Surprise, everyone!" she said, looking very spritely and jolly.

"Congratulations, people," Andrea said, holding both arms out as if she wanted to hug them all. "You made it. You are Tri Gams now."

"It was all a joke?" Nina said, looking first at Andrea, then at Mrs. Driftwood. "The whole horrible weekend was just a joke?"

"Nina, don't look so disappointed," Andrea said, annoyed. "Did you like it better when I was dead?"

"No, of course not," Nina said quickly, shaking her head. "But we were all so — scared. So miserable. I've been crying nonstop ever since we . . ."

"I guess I'm a pretty good actress," Mrs. Driftwood said, beaming, completely unaware that Nina and the others were not in an appreciative mood.

"Andrea — what was the *point*?" Rebecca asked angrily. "What was the point of frightening us like that?"

"We do it *every* year," Mrs. Driftwood declared proudly. "What a hoot!"

"We do it every year," Andrea repeated. "It's a test. A test of . . . courage . . . I guess. You can't just walk in and be a Tri Gam, you know. You've got to *earn* it. Now, come on, people. Cheer up. You've all earned it. You're all going to be Tri Gams now!"

Andrea was obviously disappointed by the silent response this news brought. "Well . . . I know it'll take a little while for the shock to wear off," she said, forcing her smile back. "This happens every year. But I just want to say how proud I am and . . . uh . . ."

Nina jumped to her feet and stepped up to Andrea, a determined look on her face. "I . . .

uh . . . this may sound stupid, but I'm going to say it anyway," Nina said, unable to keep the anger from her voice.

"I — I just want to say how disappointed I am, how hurt and disappointed at — at *everything*! You know, Andrea, I wanted to be a Tri Gam more than anything else in the world. To belong, to be part of a group. Not just any group — but the *best* group. That's what I wanted to be for *once* in my life. I . . . I was even willing to commit a crime to be able to join that group. Isn't that amazing?

"Well . . . I — I'm not just disappointed that the Tri Gams would pull this stupid prank on their pledges. I'm not just hurt. I'm ashamed. I'm ashamed of the Tri Gams. I'm ashamed of myself." Nina stared hard into Andrea's eyes. "That's all I have to say."

Andrea looked away. "Well, Nina, I'm sorry," she said, almost in a whisper. "If you don't want to join the Tri Gams —"

"Wait a minute —" Nina interrupted. "I didn't say that, Andrea. I'm joining the Tri Gams. I'm not walking away. I earned my place this weekend. I'm not giving it up."

Andrea looked confused. "But you just said —"

"I'm going to be a Tri Gam, Andrea," Nina said, growing more confident as she spoke. "And I'm going to see to it that it *does* become the best sorority on campus. And the first thing I'm going to fight for is to get rid of this awful weekend you make your pledges go through every year!"

"Fine, Nina. Fine," Andrea said, backing toward the stairs. "It was just a joke, you know. You'll all survive. . . ." She turned to go upstairs.

"Wait a minute, Andrea!" Leila called. "What about Abby? Abby *didn't* survive your little joke."

Andrea's mouth opened in surprise. She looked down to the floor, seeing Abby for the first time. "Oh, my God. What happened to her?"

"It's a long story," Leila said softly. "We've got to get help for her."

Andrea blushed. "I'm sorry. Yes, of course. We'll phone for help — immediately. Come on." She begun running to the stairs.

"There *is* a phone?" Nina called.

"Yes. It's hidden in the upstairs linen closet," Andrea called back, already halfway up the stairs. Mrs. Driftwood and the other girls followed.

Nina bent down and took Abby's hand. "Do you want to come upstairs?" she asked softly.

"I'm not Abby. I'm Gabriella."

"Can you stand up, Gabriella? Or do you want to stay here?" Nina asked her.

"I'm not Abby. I'm Gabriella."

"Is there anything I can do to help?"

Startled, Nina looked up to see Jessie

standing above her, looking very concerned. "Do you want me to help carry her upstairs?" Jessie asked.

"I don't think we'd better," Nina replied.

"I'm not Abby. I'm Gabriella."

"We'd better just stay with her here until help arrives," Nina said. "Hey — Jessie — "

"What?"

"I don't get it. In the antiques store, we all watched you examine Mrs. Driftwood. You said she was dead. And then . . . I remember it so clearly . . . *you* were the one who examined Andrea up in her room. And you said she was dead. . . ."

Jessie grinned. "I guess you figured it out, Sherlock."

"You mean — "

"That's right," Jessie said. "I was in on the joke. You see, my big sister was a Tri Gam. And she told me about this stunt the Tri Gams pull every year with their pledges. Andrea knew I knew. So. . . ."

"So you knew it was all just a put-on the whole time."

Jessie's smile faded. "I tried to tell you not to take it so seriously, Nina, not to be so upset," she said. "I tried to — "

"But you *saw* how upset I was," Nina cried, growing angrier the more she thought about it. "And you saw how scared everyone was. How *could* you, Jessie? How could you keep on with the joke when you saw how awful we all felt?"

Jessie shrugged. "What choice did I have?" she asked. "I gave my word to Andrea and the other officers." Then she quickly added, "Besides, it's all over now. Tri Gam pledges go through the same thing every year, you know. It's not like you're the first or anything."

"Yes. But —"

Jessie made a face. "Next I suppose you'll blame *me* for Abby here."

"No, Jessie. You're not to blame for Abby." It was Leila who had replied. She had been standing there with Gordon all along.

"I'm not Abby," Abby said from her kneeling position on the floor. She seemed dazed, unable to focus or comprehend what was happening.

"*I'm* to blame for Abby," Leila said, tears forming in the corners of her eyes. "I — I guess I — " She couldn't hold it all back any longer. The tears that began to slide down Lelia's cheeks unleashed a flood of emotion.

Leila fell to her knees beside Abby, sobbing loudly. She wrapped her arms around Abby and hugged her in a tight embrace. "You were my best friend. My best friend," Leila said. She began to pet Abby's smooth, black hair.

Abby stared at the wall.

"I'm so sorry," Leila said through her tears. "I'm so sorry, Abby. Can you hear me? I never wanted this to happen. Never.

We were such good friends. Such friends. Can you hear me?"

Tears formed in Abby's eyes, too. Leila began to laugh. She was laughing and crying, laughing and crying. It felt good to let it all out. And maybe — maybe she was getting through to Abby.

Tenderly, Leila continued to pet Abby's hair. She began to feel a little better, a little calmer. It was good to unburden all that guilt, all that grief she had held in for so long. Now she felt lighter than air. She stopped crying.

"Leila, you really can't blame yourself for what's happened to Abby," Nina said softly, putting her hand on Leila's shoulder.

Leila smiled up at her.

They heard the high wail of an approaching siren. "That's probably an ambulance for Abby," Leila said. "I guess Andrea reached someone."

"Go on upstairs. You've had a terrible scare," Nina told Leila. "I'll wait here until they come for Abby."

"Okay," Leila said. "Goodbye, Abby. Goodbye. I'll see you real soon."

Gordon gently pulled Leila to her feet and led her up the stairs. A few moments later, they were standing in the living room, staring into the fireplace at the ragged carpet of glowing red embers, remains of the dying fire.

Leila took Gordon's hands in hers and squeezed them tightly. His hands were warm.

Hers were cold as ice. She had the feeling she would never get them warm.

"I must look a mess," she said, blowing a strand of hair from her eyes.

"I've seen you look better," Gordon said, and then laughed.

"I want to go away," she said, pressing her forehead against his shoulder.

"Away? Where?" He lowered his head to kiss her forehead.

"Nowhere. Anywhere. I don't know. Home, I guess. Home to take a long, hot bath."

He smiled. "Then what?"

"Then I'm going to go to classes, and work hard, and have fun. And I'm going to forget all about the Tri Gams."

"Whoa!" He backed away from her. "What did you say? What do you mean? You *are* a Tri Gam now."

"Well . . . I'm quitting," Leila said.

"Quitting?"

"Yeah. I don't want to be a Tri Gam. I mean it." She stared down at the warm embers. "I just want to be with you."

Gordon's shocked expression turned to a pleased smile. "You're serious!" he said. "I don't believe you! You went through this whole horrible weekend. You made it. And now you're quitting?"

"You heard me," Leila told him, pulling him close again. "Quitting."

He grinned at her. "You really are

twisted . . ." he said, lowering his head to kiss her lips ". . . but I'm glad."

Two paramedics in white lab coats walked quickly across the basement floor to help Abby up. They stopped a few feet away from her. She didn't seem to notice them. All of her attention was on her sister.

"Gabriella — I asked you not to embarrass me," Abby scolded, sounding more weary than angry.

"I didn't embarrass you," Gabriella replied in her throaty voice. "I protected you."

"But the other pledges. . . . What will they think?" Abby asked, staring around the basement, not focusing on anything.

"I warned you, Abby, not to pledge the sorority," Gabriella said. "You and I don't belong in a sorority."

"But we're not the same person, Gabriella," Abby protested weakly. "You've got to let me live my own life."

"Of course, dear," Gabriella said. "I only want to protect you. That's the only reason I'm here."

The paramedics gently helped Abby to her feet and led her into the ambulance.

"What's happening?" Abby cried, her voice tightening in alarm. "What are they doing? Where are they taking me?"

"Don't worry, dear sister," Gabriella purred. "You'll be okay." A wide grin spread across her face. "I'm coming along, too."

About the Author

R.L. STINE is the author of more than ninety books of humor, adventure, and mystery for young readers. He has written more than twenty thrillers such as this one.

In addition to his publishing work, he is headwriter of the children's TV show *Eureeka's Castle*, seen on Nickelodeon.

He lives in New York City with his wife, Jane, and their son, Matt.

THRILLERS

Nobody Scares 'Em Like
R.L. Stine

☐	BAJ44236-8	The Baby-sitter	$3.50
☐	BAJ44332-1	The Baby-sitter II	$3.50
☐	BAJ46099-4	The Baby-sitter III	$3.50
☐	BAJ45386-6	Beach House	$3.50
☐	BAJ43278-8	Beach Party	$3.50
☐	BAJ43125-0	Blind Date	$3.50
☐	BAJ43279-6	The Boyfriend	$3.50
☐	BAJ44333-X	The Girlfriend	$3.50
☐	BAJ45385-8	Hit and Run	$3.25
☐	BAJ46100-1	Hitchhiker	$3.50
☐	BAJ43280-X	The Snowman	$3.50
☐	BAJ43139-0	Twisted	$3.50

Available wherever you buy books, or use this order form.

point ® # THRILLERS

R.L. Stine

- ☐ MC44236-8 The Baby-sitter — $3.50
- ☐ MC44332-1 The Baby-sitter II — $3.50
- ☐ MC45386-6 Beach House — $3.25
- ☐ MC43278-8 Beach Party — $3.50
- ☐ MC43125-0 Blind Date — $3.50
- ☐ MC43279-6 The Boyfriend — $3.50
- ☐ MC44333-X The Girlfriend — $3.50
- ☐ MC45385-8 Hit and Run — $3.25
- ☐ MC46100-1 The Hitchhiker — $3.50
- ☐ MC43280-X The Snowman — $3.50
- ☐ MC43139-0 Twisted — $3.50

Caroline B. Cooney

- ☐ MC44316-X The Cheerleader — $3.25
- ☐ MC41641-3 The Fire — $3.25
- ☐ MC43806-9 The Fog — $3.25
- ☐ MC45681-4 Freeze Tag — $3.25
- ☐ MC45402-1 The Perfume — $3.25
- ☐ MC44884-6 The Return of the Vampire — $2.95
- ☐ MC41640-5 The Snow — $3.25
- ☐ MC45682-2 The Vampire's Promise — $3.50

Diane Hoh

- ☐ MC44330-5 The Accident — $3.25
- ☐ MC45401-3 The Fever — $3.25
- ☐ MC43050-5 Funhouse — $3.25
- ☐ MC44904-4 The Invitation — $3.50
- ☐ MC45640-7 The Train (9/92) — $3.25

Sinclair Smith

- ☐ MC45063-8 The Waitress — $2.95

Christopher Pike

- ☐ MC43014-9 Slumber Party — $3.50
- ☐ MC44256-2 Weekend — $3.50

A. Bates

- ☐ MC45829-9 The Dead Game — $3.25
- ☐ MC43291-5 Final Exam — $3.25
- ☐ MC44582-0 Mother's Helper — $3.50
- ☐ MC44238-4 Party Line — $3.25

D.E. Athkins

- ☐ MC45246-0 Mirror, Mirror — $3.25
- ☐ MC45349-1 The Ripper — $3.25
- ☐ MC44941-9 Sister Dearest — $2.95

Carol Ellis

- ☐ MC44768-8 My Secret Admirer — $3.25
- ☐ MC46044-7 The Stepdaughter — $3.25
- ☐ MC44916-8 The Window — $2.95

Richie Tankersley Cusick

- ☐ MC43115-3 April Fools — $3.25
- ☐ MC43203-6 The Lifeguard — $3.25
- ☐ MC43114-5 Teacher's Pet — $3.25
- ☐ MC44235-X Trick or Treat — $3.25

Lael Littke

- ☐ MC44237-6 Prom Dress — $3.25

Edited by T. Pines

- ☐ MC45256-8 Thirteen — $3.50

Available wherever you buy books, or use this order form.

Scholastic Inc., P.O. Box 7502, 2931 East McCarty Street, Jefferson City, MO 65102

Please send me the books I have checked above. I am enclosing $ _____ (please add $2.00 to cover shipping and handling). Send check or money order — no cash or C.O.D.s please.

Name _____

Address_____

City _____ State/Zip _____

Please allow four to six weeks for delivery. Offer good in the U.S. only. Sorry, mail orders are not available to residents of Canada. Prices subject to change.   PT1092